HITTAZ 4

AS GRIMEY AS IT GETS

LOU GARDEN PRICE, SR.

URBAN AINT DEAD

Search Lou Garden Price SBI #00454309

James T Vaughn Correctional Center, Smyrna DELAWARE

For tablet connection. Download the gettingout.com app.

Contact Publisher at www.urbanaintdead.com

Email: urbanaintdead@gmail.com

Print ISBN: 979-8-9886522-7-4

CONTENTS

SOUNDTRACKS

Scan the QR Code below to listen to the Soundtracks/Singles of some of your favorite U.A.D titles:

Don't have Spotify or Apple Music?
No Sweat!
Visit your choice streaming platform and search URBAN AINT DEAD.

Currently on lock serving a bid?
JPay, iHeartRadio, WHATEVER!
We got you covered.

Simply log into your facility's kiosk or tablet, go to music and
search URBAN AINT DEAD.

URBAN AINT DEAD

SUBMISSIONS

Submit the first three chapters of your completed manuscript to <u>urbanaintdead@gmail.com</u>, subject line: Your book's title. The manuscript must be in a .doc file and sent as an attachment. The document should be in Times New Roman, double-spaced, and in size 12 font. Also, provide your synopsis and full contact information. If sending multiple submissions, they must each be in a separate email. Have a story but no way to submit it electronically? You can still submit to URBAN AINT DEAD. Send in the first three chapters, written or typed, of your completed manuscript to:

URBAN AINT DEAD
P.O Box 448
Maybrook, NY 12543

DO NOT send original manuscript. Must be a duplicate.
Provide your synopsis and a cover letter containing your full contact information.
Thanks for considering URBAN AINT DEAD.

FOREWORD

Every normal man must be tempted,

At times, to spit on his hands, hoist the black flag, and begin

slitting throats.

H.L. Mencken

CHAPTER ONE

Mid-West Hummer

Monday 11:00 AM

"This fucking COVID-19 is like a goddamn sore in the ass crack that never goes away," the dark skin, twenty-nine-year-old Black N9NE said to China Man, AKA Monk, as they sat inside the Mid-West Hummer dealership in Chicago's downtown area.

"Yeah, I know," Monk nodded as he texted. "Boo had it, then Knarf… and right now Uzenna's tested positive!"

Currently with N9NE and Monk inside the showroom floor of the dealership was Fast Eddie Kane, Ground War, and several of Joker Red's wives: Julia, Melodie, Louise, and Diane, who also had six-month-old babies with them.

The Everything Is Everything or EIE, organization was at the Hummer dealership to order a fleet of brand-new custom-made Hummers. The women were there to deliver Joker Red's orders to the owner of the prestigious dealership, which contained specific details of the custom work he wanted done on each luxury vehicle. This fleet would not all be the same color, and not all have the same level of bullet/bomb proofing as the Cadillac fleet.

"I'm coverin' the wives, kids, and core EIE only," Joker had told Julia and Melodie just that morning. If mother-fuckers like Rebel, Blackbird, or Devastator want to up the level of armor on the Hummers I give 'em... they can feel free. I'm *givin'* 'em the truck. I'm not paying a quarter million for armor on each one. Everybody has their own money."

As they all left the dealership, Melodie laughed and said, "I don't care about all the armor, girl, just give me the truck!"

"They are beautiful," Julia emphasized as they walked toward where they had a Range Rover and Cadillac SUV parked out front of the dealership.

A brown van was parked in the space to the left of Melodie's white Range Rover. To the immediate right of the Range Rover was the blue Cadillac. And on its immediate right sat a shuttle bus with tinted windows. Ground War, a seasoned combat veteran, never missed anything...

"Hold!" Ground War drew his MP-5 and caused the other soldiers to do the same. "The brown van! I'll take the bus!" They spread out.

Mark, N9NE, Mustafa, Ground War, and Eddie slowly

approached the two suspicious vans but, seconds later, determined that all was clear.

"You scared me!" Melodie said to Ground War. "Fuck, man, the war is over!" She admonished him.

"Two vans boxing us in…" Ground War shrugged. "Looks suspicious."

They opened the doors to their vehicles, and as they were strapping the babies into their car seats, it happened. The explosion of the brown van on the left and a second – more devastating – blast of the shuttle bus to the right! The force of both bombs, with the shrapnel of glass, shards of metal, and other deadly incendiary debris, ripped through everyone caught up in the horrible hellfire!

Monk, Black N9NE, Big Chief, Fast Eddie Kane, Mustafa, Ground War, Julia, Melodie Louise, Diane, and their four babies – Joker Red's children – all were assassinated by an enemy's bombs!

The babies were dead inside their car seats. Everyone else was lying burned and shredded on the ground, also deceased. The devices would later be identified as two C-4 types, packed with nails, nuts, bolts, and ball bearings for maximum human devastation.

This most certainly looked like a targeted assassination attempt on Joker Red's life that ended the lives of some of his closest comrades, his gorgeous wives, and most of all, his beautiful babies.

CHAPTER TWO

Don Frank Braga and his younger brother (and underboss) Vinnie "The Butcher" Braga were among the first to arrive at the executive luxury "Twin Towers" building of EIE HQ and extend their condolences.

"Red," Don Frank said as he sat beside him on the balcony. I'm destroyed with you, my son." The Don had tears of sorrow in his eyes.

Those tender words from a much older Don Frank to Joker were needed more than he knew. Because right now, Joker was destroyed and only a "fatherly" type like Don

Frank could understand this void… this ultra inflammatory anger Joker felt. Saying "my son" evoked waterworks to start pouring from the gangster's eyes.

"That means a lot," Joker was nearly breathless as he tried to choke back his sobs.

Vinnie stood nearby with his hands thrust deeply inside of his pants pockets. "I'm very sorry for your losses, J.R."

Inside the house the shrill screams and cries of Uzenna and the other wives could be heard. The men paused with their heads heavy, staring at the ground. News of what had occurred had already made the rounds among EIE members, and everybody was now at Joker Red's house.

"Ghostman's here," Iani opened the door to announce before reclosing it.

Moments later, Ghostman came out onto the balcony. He immediately embraced his comrade with a powerful grip.

"We know anything?" Ghostman asked.

"Not yet," Don Braga said.

"But we will," Joker added. Between the Dons officials and our intelligence resources… there's no way possible not to find out who was behind this."

"Starting with all the cameras at and around the Hummer dealer," Big Frank said.

"I have specific people out there collectin' every image available," Joker revealed angrily. "That footage and every scrap and component left behind by those two car bombs will be analyzed by the CIA, DOD, and FBI. And I'm gonna know somethin'… then, it's Armageddon."

Ghostman's Mansion
Tuesday 2:45 PM

GHOSTMAN DINERO WAS ON EDGE. HE COULDN'T SHOW IT around Joker, but once he exited the Twin Towers and hopped inside his all-black Bugatti, he slammed his hand on the steering wheel several times. A minute later, he drove off, heading to his Winthrop Harbor, Illinois, mansion.

On the open highway, he reached speeds of up to 180 mph, not caring about being stopped because there wasn't a police car in America that could ever catch him. Nevertheless, he made it home in no time. He was waved through by his own hired "PMC" (private military company) soldiers who were not affiliated with EIE. They were all heavily armed and wore tactical gear, covering all areas of the sprawling estate.

Ghostman loved his luxury cars, and he owned ten of them now. They were all parked on the gleaming white lime-stone circular deck out in front of the massive 24-room mansion: a black Ferrari Enzo, a Canary Lamborghini Gallardo, a Pepsi blue Aston Martin Vanquish, a charcoal Rolls-Royce Phantom, a white Acura, a silver Lincoln Navigator SSE, a black fully automatic Range Rover, his trusty blue bomb proofed Cadillac SUV, a red Charger with insane racing stripes and the 1000-horsepower Bugatti he was pulling up in now.

A large black man with a bald head met Ghostman at the side of the house.

"Simon," Ghostman greeted him. "What up wit it?"

"Boss." Simon tilted his head towards the house. "The missus has several visitors inside."

Ghostman looked at all the vehicles parked outside among his and Honey B's cars. "I see. Who are they?"

"Four men, four women," Simon shrugged. "No weapons, no digital devices. Not that they didn't have any."

Ghostman nodded and started to leave.

"One more thing," Simon said. "They are Mexican except for one female. She's a right lady with an unmistakable accent."

"Accent? English?"

Simon shook his head. "Albanian."

"Hm," Ghostman scowled. "Thanks, Simon."

Inside the house, Ghostman walked into the living room where Honey B was dressed in a stylish grey and black Prada dress and black knee-high leather boots. She was holding the glass of wine in one hand while talking in fast Spanish, waving her other hand animatedly as she got her point across to her eight guests.

"Daddy, there you are!" She lit up when she saw him. "Lemme introduce you to…"

He cut her off by holding his pointer finger up to his lips. He walked over to the entertainment system and turned the music softly playing on volume two up to volume eight. Then he went up to her and hugged her tightly, his mouth close to her ear.

"We have to be extra careful," he said as her guests watched. The music drowned out his voice. "The nigga is using the Don's police and political power in the city. The cameras on the ground will be analyzed by the CIA, DOD and the FBI. And the bombs will be chemically and forensically analyzed… most likely in Washington."

She stopped him, turned down the music and said to her guests, Sorry. This is my husband, Ghostman Dinero. Ghost let's just say that these are *our* friends from Mexico. Excuse us for a few minutes."

She followed him out into the backyard, where they stood at the far-right side of the swimming pools deepened.

"Okay," she started by placing a calming hand against his chest. "We have to remain focused no matter what. Why are you so worked up?"

"I *told* you," he lowered his voice.

She smirked and shrugged her shoulders. "We did what we set out to do – we savagely broke his heart."

Ghostman shook his head. "But you never said we was takin' out my own crew!" He nearly shouted.

"That's not the plan," she whispered. "Who do you think will kill us if they ever suspect us? Those soldiers were casualties of war," she reasoned.

The Hummer dealership bombing was a well thought out, well executed plan made possible only because of how close Ghostman was to those around Joker. However, Honey B did not use Ghostman to set up bombs or the vehicles used in the bombings.

"I hope your people know what you they're doing, he took a deep breath and exhaled or we're all fuckin' dead."

"Papi," she stated assuringly. "When I told you to let me have the wheel… J.R.'s fate was sealed – in Hell."

"That was *six months* ago," he reminded her.

"And look," she held his hand to her protruding belly. "Your son will be here soon. You are my husband now. And we have amassed money Joker cannot call EIE's."

"By dealing with friends of El Verdugo's."

She frowned. "You mean *enemies* of El Verdugo's."

"Hm." He tilted his head towards the house. "Who are they?"

"Powerful friends of ours," Honey B told him. "C'mon. Lemme introduce you."

"No." He stopped short. "He's using CIA resources. What if we're bugged?"

She was annoyed. "We knew the power he has goin' in. We are wired to the teeth here. No one is surveillin' us except us, stupid! Besides we are going to talk about the national tattoo shop chain, the white girls and Mexican cartel meth we'll need out West."

"White girls," he repeated.

She paused. "White girls. Blancitas. The slaves."

He hesitated. "The Albanian woman. That's why she's here."

The Camilla Cabello looking Latina stared at him. "I never said Albanian…"

"Sex slaves?"

"Simon," she figured it out quickly. "You gonna let me

take the wheel or are we gonna flush millions of dollars down the toilet?"

"We not flushin' anything mamai," he told her. "I just need you to keep in mind that we dealin' wit a nigga from the hood who ain't no ordinary nigga. He a genius. He think he fuckin' invincible."

"Every but of intel we had put him at that Hummer dealership," Honey sighed. "So maybe he invincible or at least very hard ti kill."

"That was good luck for him and bad luck for us," Ghost stated, shrugging, reaching for her and kissing her. He squeezed her soft ass through her sexy dress. "I wish I could fuck you right now."

"Me too, Papi. Let's get this meeting done and you can even grab the Astroglide. You been wantin' to bone me all up my ass for a week!" She smiled flirtatiously with him. "I see how you been looking at it."

"Bone it, kiss it, lick it, smell it, spank it."

He followed her on into the house.

CHAPTER THREE

Joker's Penthouse
Tuesday 3:00 PM

No matter what it is, with every good or bad decision one makes, there is always a "balance due."

Uzenna and her twelve "sisters" had been manipulated and forced into living their lives as sex slaves for an Italian criminal enterprise for years as minors but were eventually freed by an even more formidable gangster. While Joker Red's will and desire to save the 13 women was extremely heroic at that time... Uzenna realized that her decision to unite her life and lead her girls into combining their lives with Joker Red had a balance due. A terrible price to pay.

"I killed my own sister," Uzenna whispered from the guest bedroom she was isolating in because she contracted the Omicron variant of COVID-19.

Romie was killed after it had been discovered that she was having a torrid sexual affair with A-Son – one of Joker's top men. Inside of EIE, Joker was boss of all bosses, and since Uzenna was his wife, that made her boss of all bitches.

Including her own blood – her baby sister Romie. So, she had made the top bitch "OG call" that Romie had to be executed to preserve everything they had built. The other twelve sister-wives, thirteen when newcomer Indian goddess Tithi Patel was counted – needed to maintain the trust of Joker and the entire EIE, who believed in what he had created.

Oddly enough, having and holding down over a dozen young wives – not to mention impregnating all of them – added to Red's legendary "superpower" and mastery as the organization's leader. For one of the wives to betray him like that without paying the most severe – albeit permanent – penalty might show weakness. Uzenna had thought she could fix the betrayal if she were to be the one to deliver the punishment, however…

Since the day of Romie's death, Uzenna had had nightmares over what she had done to her sister. Romie had begged and pleaded with Uzenna to spare her life but, instead, Uzenna had shed Romie's blood. Something Uzenna had vowed never to do to her own sisters.

"What will the balance due be?" Uzenna said aloud as she

paced back and forth barefoot across the carpet. *"There has to be more…"*

She was on her seventh day of self-quarantine because of the positive test result of the COVID-19 rapid test she had taken. She was extremely shaken over the bombing assassinations.

"Diane, Loulou (Louise), *Mel* (Melodie), *Jules* (Julia)," Uzenna shook her head sadly. *"And those four precious babies. And not the new EIE soldiers but the core cats: N9NE, China Man, War and Staf (Mufastfa)). Is that it? How many more of us has to die?"* She asked aloud.

She was so upset she was freaking out.

"Red!!" She yelled at the top of her lungs. *"Red!! Somebody get Red goddammit!!"* She demanded.

Tithi came to the door. "You okay, Butterfly?"

"Is your fuckin' name Red, bitch?!" Uzenna snapped as she snatched the door open. "Is it?!"

"N-no, I…" Tithi stepped back, not wanting COVID-19.

"I said somebody get me Red!!"

Joker walked down the hallway after several of his women called him. He put on his N-95 mask and told Tithi, "Go."

"Who fuckin' did this?!" Uzenna shouted. "Who assassinated twelve of ours in one shot?! In the streets?!"

She had tears on top of tears spilling down her face like a waterfall, snot coming out of her nose and drool dribbling out of her mouth. Joker could only think of coronavirus at the sight of all those bodily fluids on her face.

He closed the door and walked over to the large windows

which were rear-facing the swimming pool and immaculately kept grounds below. He opened both windows with a turn crank that allowed the windows to swing outwards, letting air in.

He sat down and thrust his hands into his black hoodie. "You need to calm down."

"What?!" she exploded. "A dozen of our people lie burnt to a crisp, blown to fuckin' *McNuggets*... and y'all out there *lollipoppin'* and frowning, with five-thousand-dollar bottles of Courvoisier open!!"

He stared a hole into her.

He stood up and exited the room.

"Yeah, leave!!" She screamed at him. "Leave!!"

He spun around. *"I told you to calm down!"*

"*Fuck* calming down!" She spat, enraged. "I should have calmed down and rethought not killin' Romie! That's how I should have calmed down!"

He grabbed her by her arms and shook her violently. "Whattaya sayin'? Hm?"

"I said it!" She hissed, trying to wrestle her arms loose. "I never should have put you before my baby sister! This so-called <u>family</u> we have! You don't care about us like *we* care about us!" She accused him.

"I don't?" He retorted in a growl. "If not for me you'd still be dancin' for dollar bills and suckin' the white man's weiner in his stinky office!"

"If not for you?" She laughed in his face. "What did *you* do?"

He released her. A group of his people had got together in the hallway outside the guest bedroom door.

"You've been taken them fuckin' Zannies and drinkin'," he realized.

"Man," she scoffed. "Ain't nothin' slow about me. You talkin' 'bout *'if not for me.'* You… what*tayu* do? Order others to do the gangster work? You, on the other hand, take no risks."

Iani had heard enough. She barged in to save what Uzenna's mouth was ripping apart. "Sis, be quiet. Daddy, you go cool off."

"Nah, Iani," Uzenna said heatedly. "He needs to know… I'm saying what we have all been thinking! We killed Romie – For this? For a coward?"

"Shut! The! Fuck! Up!" Iani shouted as she walked Uzenna into the bathroom. "C'mon. You got snot in yout nose."

"Just great, Zen, you just signed our death warrant wit your big fat fuckin' mouth!" Iani hissed. "We're dead."

"You don't get it, do you, Ani?" Uzenna spoke in the saddest, most lost and defeated tone Iani had ever heard from anyone. She sounded literally like life was over.

"Get what? You bein' selfish and you talkin' fuckin' stupid!" Iani was mad at her. "You wanna end it then put a fuckin' blaster in your mouth and get ta eatin' it bitch! Don't kill the rest of us becuz you havin' regrets!"

"He never ever intended for any of this to have a happy ending!" Uzenna yelled back at her older sister. "He manipulated us the whole way just like the rest. Our father, our aunts, uncles, them bastards who bought us, then sold us to the New York Brooklyn people. We just been gettin' *fucked* We're still hos – just a new kinda ho. And look we killed our own sister – somethin' we swore we'd never do."

"Look you dumb bitch," Iani pointed to the rock on Uzenna's finger. "More than a million dollars on your wedding band and engagement wit millions more in the bank. You're the true wife so miss me with it. You got da best deal out of all of us and you're burning it to da ground."

Joker had left in a cold-blooded mood. He planned right then to kill Uzenna. He just didn't know exactly how yet.

CHAPTER FOUR

Ghostman's Mansion
Tuesday 5:00 PM

Her name was Valoria.

At 5 foot 11 inches, she was tall for a woman. She was slim, with nectarine breasts, a very squeezable little ass, her black hair fell to the center of her back and reminded one of a Pantene shampoo commercial because it looked so luxurious and clean all the time. Nothing was out of place on this woman. Even her thick eyebrows fit in perfectly with her squarish face, dimpled chin, and silvery gray eyes.

Ghostman was intrigued by her. "You look like a super-model," he complemented her.

The thirty-eight-year-old Albanian woman frowned. "Those stuck-up beeches?" She spoke with a heavy Eastern European accent. Ghostman learned that she was from a city in Albania called Durrés. A bustling resort metropolis that sat on the shores of the Adriatic Sea between Tirane and to the north Elbasan to the Southeast.

Ghostman poured her all the expensive Ace of Spades champagne she could drink as they sat inside the cozy bottom level living room. He loved listening to such a "different" kind of high crime figure speak. She was very sophisticated, and despite the mud and dirty poverty she came from she was well-educated.

"Were you sold into slavery?" Ghostman asked her.

She stared at him. "I was never foolish girl. Just like I will never be foolish woman. How about *I* pour… *you* drink?" She asked with a sly smile.

Ghostman chuckled. "That what you think? I'm tryna get you to drink so you can talk?"

"My father was an Albanian Besa mobster," she said. "He discovered there was a plot to kill him by fellow mobsters, so he betrayed his honor by ratting them out to police. I was nine when one of the betrayed men kidnapped me out of revenge and sold me to a local sex trafficker."

"At age nine," Ghostman shook his head.

Valoria nodded. "But I immediately escaped from them before I could be placed into a shipping container and sent to America. I returned to my father…"

"How'd that go?" Ghost wanted to know.

"I demanded he tell me why he turned rat," she stated, downing the entire glass of fine champagne.

Ghost smirked. "A snitch never tells the truth. What did his snitching ass say?"

"He said very little," she said as Ghost poured them another round. "He savagely beat me… and we went on the run. First Algiers and then to Barcelona. He raped me, I was his daily sperm deposit at nine years old. I became pregnant, miscarried, and he never quit. Each day I was raped but when we went to Morocco, I became an expert at pleasing a man."

"All at age nine?"

"By age eleven," she revealed. "My father robbed and killed with guns and our money grew. He had men in Casablanca and Spain he'd organized, and we returned to Albania when I was fifteen, with two of his children. He started war with Albania mobsters, and it looked like he would be victor."

Ghostman was all into the story. "It looked like; whattaya mean?" He inquired.

"Big shootout at our doorstep," she said matter of factly. "Until I came out with my hands up… Telling all his men… And his enemies… That I put a double barrel shotgun to his back and squeeze both triggers."

Honey Bee, her four Mexican guests and the other three Mexican ladies entered the room just then.

"Oh shit!" He said as he barely glanced at the beautiful Mexican ladies. "It was fuckin' *you*?"

"For six years, I was a sex slave to that demon and had his

two bastard children," she spat. "In both pregnancies I felt hatred for hees demons seeds. So, once he was dead, we became united. We are NJË which means one."

"So," he stopped her. "His Morocco men – they didn't want to kill you?"

She admitted a cynical laugh. "I was beautiful young girl. They see pretty eyes, full mouth, I tease and show pink tipped nipples, sweet little pussy... and the manipulation began. They *knew* that I would kill him... and that same night... I *drowned* his two incest demon retards in the bathtub of our flat."

Honey B was shocked for the children. She looked at Ghost.

He glanced at Valoria and the other men and women in the room. Youse a regular bad ass bitch, huh?"

Valoria shrugged it off. "Killing makes me feel... *happy*. I mean, some people eat ice cream, have sex, or go to petting zoo to make them happy. Me?... I look for enemy and kill my enemy to make me happy."

"I'm gonna love her, B," Ghost told his woman.

"I knew you would," Honey Bee smiled. "Everyone in this room is a killer. But that is not why we're here. First, meet the ladies: Helena, Laila and Nobi are here on behalf of Tijuana cartel. Thank you and Nico, Aurelio, Juan, and Kiko of the Gulf cartel. Both the Tijuana and Gulf cartels despise El Verdugo because he was hired to assassinate many members of their families."

Ghostman looked around. "And y'all here, and your

peoples, knows my wife – y'all have no beef with her?" He wanted clarity.

Kiko, the curly haired Gulf cartel representative shook his head. "None. We are not bringing attention to you. We try to find a way back into Chicago and this major meth distro she offered."

His other three men nodded.

The three ladies repeated pretty much the same thing. No one wanted war.

"Tijuana and Gulf was not involved in the war you have like El Verdugo," Aurelio added. "We were at war with him, Los Zetas, and Aztecas."

Ghostman nodded, satisfied.

"Your wife has a child with El Verdugo," Helena pointed out. "Our sworn enemy is the Juarez cartel who he worked for. But times have changed – she is a woman with power. She asked us for a third element. So, we've brought it," she declared.

"Third element," Ghostman repeated.

"Tijuana, Gulf…" Helena nodded towards the Valoria. "Number three: The Albanians."

"But this sex trafficking…" Ghostman exhaled, shaking his head. "I'm not a fan… and neither is our nemesis."

"That's only the surface," Valoria told him. "You use strippers to promote your crystal meth inside of underground clubs and criminal networks. We do the same only with heroin and coke we buy from our Mexican friends."

Helena spoke up. "And we know that EIE has a hard time keeping up with the demand for meth due to a regulation by the DEA of necessary ingredients needed to manufacture meth."

"Ephedrine and pseudoephedrine," Ghost nodded. "Our main meth cook has contacts out west and among farmers in the South, so we do well."

"Well enough to cover the dark web and all of America?" Helena asked. "Come on now. We're here because you know you can't do it alone."

"That all you here for?" Ghostman smooth shot back.

There was a pause.

"That's why we're having this meeting, Papi," Honey said. "Everything will be made clear."

Ghostman relaxed. "Aight… Lay it all out…"

CHAPTER FIVE

The Twin Towers
Tuesday 6:30 PM

"What are y'all bitches out here huddlin' in about?" Iani inquired as she stepped into the hallway to smoke some weed.

Coral, Ashley, Leah, Eden, Valerie, and Brittani were already out there. Some of them were passing around blunts and others cigarettes. No smoking inside of their homes anymore since the children had come along.

Brittani – the Alexis Texas look alike – spoke up first. "Never seen Uzenna go off on him like that." She said.

"We ain't rubber-stampin' that shit she was saying," Coral stated. "Frankly, I'm scared to death of his reaction."

"She went too far," Leah added.

"So y'all gonna just bad mouth her?" Iani defended Uzenna. "That's our sister!" She reminded them. Only she could talk bad about her sister,

Valarie put her hand on her hip. When she going off the deep end like that, she ain't!"

"Y'all some ungrateful ass hoes," Iani accused. "And remember: y'all is *still* hoes. Uzenna rode wit all of us. Some of you nasty garbage bag bitches was wearin' the same stinking sperm-stained panties when youse met us. Now what Uzenna did I cussed her out about already cuz it put us all in jeopardy of losing everything. Including our lives. But y'all bitches ain't got no right to be turning on my baby sister for shit. Especially what with the way we found y'all. We upgraded y'all hoes."

"We ended up being pimped by the mob," Valerie said with her face contorted in anger. "You glorifying that shit?"

"Bitch you was thirteen getin' gang banged for a bologna sandwich and a place to sleep," Iani reminded her. "You were givin' your snatch away until we brought you into a better way."

"We are still loyal, but we have a blood pact with him," Brittani interjected. "You can bite and scratch all you want but we have babies to look out for now. And he's their fuckin' father. I love the shit out of Zen, and I love Red, too… But my son with him is everything. This family is everything and that shit she was saying was foul. I'm standing with Red."

Eden spoke up in her own quiet way. "No one's choosin' a side… We are all a family. These babies changed it all. Romie chose betrayal – she paid… Ash could choose to abandon ship… You and Uzenna could choose to abandon us… What will happen – I don't know. But twenty hours of labor – a daughter that's his *twin*? No way I'm leaving," she said adamantly.

"We all hurtin'" Ashley said as she smoked the blunt and held her breath. Then, exhaling, she stated, "Uzenna mournin' Romie still, now Loulou, Mel, Di, and Jules. Plus, she has the virus. So, she says some crazy shit. We all argue with him."

"Nah, not like that hateful shit she was saying," Brittany shook her head. "How do you survive words like that is beyond me. She felt and called him a coward for being the general of his own army."

"As if being the mastermind makes him some sort of pussy," Coral added. "You can't challenge a man's balls like that in front of his women."

"Y'all need to come on," Iani ordered them. "We need to do funeral arrangements, flowers, caskets, limmos, y'all know."

They did, indeed, know.

Death was becoming way too familiar among them.

The Twin Towers
Joker's New Penthouse

THAT EVENING, AS YOU SEND A LAY AWAKE STARING AT THE ceiling, Joker Red packed up everything he cared most about. Clothes, jewelry, files, cash, a laptop, a tablet, and many other items. He boxed them up and carried them out with Boo, Divine, Knarf, Ceasar, Bible, Devastator, Blackout, and several others.

Joker didn't want to put a spotlight on the situation, so he waited for 11:00 PM to come before he called some helping hands over. However, pretty soon, everyone in the Twin Towers knew that Joker Red was moving out of the penthouse he shared with Uzenna and into the vacant penthouse in the second building where the core group of EIE strippers lived.

Tithi, who was now working at Chicago Medical-Trauma Center was already there. She immediately began unpacking what he brought. It wasn't much.

"I'll decorate it," she promised after everyone left. "Glad it has furniture, beds, televisions."

He noisily exhaled as they relaxed on the comfortable sofa. "Yeah… When we first bought the place we furnished every unit," he recalled.

She put her small hand underneath this T-shirt and sensually massaged the rippling muscles in his belly and chest.

"You are my warrior." She kissed his abdomen. Then going lower, said: "You are my king." She kissed his pelvis as she pulled down his sweatpants, making his already hard dick spring out.

"You are an emperor." She snaked her tongue and lips along his marvelous length, wetting him. "I love how your dick and balls smell… like one hundred percent all M-A-N," she whispered.

She had him granite hard in a couple of short minutes. She made all those lovely noises as she used both her hands to suck and deep throat his enormous penis. She spit on it and took him down into her throat.

"Umm," She moaned as she fellated him.

He took off the rest of his clothing.

"Let's sixty-nine, Sweet T," he said as he peeled her tight jeans off her cinnamon brown skin. She paused to let him strip her naked.

"No shower all day, Daddy," she complained.

"You know I need it like that," he told her. "Come sit that sweet pussy and beautiful ass right here on my face while you swallow that big dick and lick all over my huge balls," he said like they were in a XXX film.

She obviously loved how demanding he was and how nasty he talked during sex. He never got tired. She hopped on top of him, backing her ass and pussy onto his face until he locked her in.

"Can you hear this?" He inhaled her deeply through his nose with his eyes closed. "Baby you smell like fresh hot buttered biscuts. You my sweet Indian goddess." He loved er musky, sea salty, aroma.

He spread her ass and pussylips apart and started eating. Her moist feminine scent took his mind off of Uzenna and the horrible deaths of his children, their mothers, and his men. At least just for a few moments. The average man would be falling apart at the seams, but Joker was no ordinary man.

The pure animalism of their heathen sex act had the Indian doctor dripping her honey cream into his face and mouth within a matter of minutes. He sucked on her clitoris while he had two fingers inside of her contracting vaginal walls and the thumb of his other hand inside of her asshole. She whimpered and then cried out in a wild series of orgasms.

He then turned her over onto her back and started fucking her slowly at first. She loved the missionary position best because she got to experience all of his big cucumber dick.

"I love the look and taste of your asshole," he whispered in her ear. "You like when I eat it and finger it?"

"Ohh, god yessss!"

"I keep dreaming of fuckin' you in your tight little asshole," he hissed forcefully in her ear. "You want me to put it in your ass?!"

"I'll do anything you want me to, Daddy," she panted as he pounded her. "Fuck my ass, baby…"

Her submissiveness made him even harder. "I love you, Doctor Patel," he declared.

She melted and her clitoris exploded first. Orgasms spread throughout her entire pussy and electric currents zapped from her brain down into her ribcage and breasts and her stomach. He picked up on her wanton pleasure when she threw her feet up onto his shoulders, inviting him to stroke his monster meat deep, deep, down into her and hit her g-spot.

"Tonight's that special night!" He gasped as he licked her

neck and ear which drove her insane. "You been wantin' it, huh?"

"I'm cummmmmmmiiiiiinnnnnngggggg!!!!!!" She whimpered and her juicy cream spilled out all over his penis and balls. "Giiimmmeee my b-bbbaaaayyybbbyyy!!!!"

Warm, wet, jets of sperm shot from his big contracting dick to splash and plant itself deep inside of the hot musky depths of her vagina and cervical walls. Even when he was done cumming inside of her she held him clamped inside of her snapper pussy, milking him, and holding him there, soothing him. She used her hands to massage his neck, shoulders, and back, all the while never breaking their close contact. She felt all of his pent-up emotions as they burst…

"Just stay inside me, Red," she whispered as he cried and sobbed his painful tears against her face and neck. "Even the strongest kings cried. You are not a weak man. You are a master, a supreme warrior, better than any other. Powerful, so good looking, a superior lovemaker…"

She had no idea how much he needed her. Or perhaps she did. Tithi was not as rough around the edges as the sister-wives and strippers he usually surrounded himself with, but she was cut from a different cloth nonetheless.

When she heard him finally sleeping, she was relieved. She stayed connected with him all night and through the morning hours… Her body soothing, calming, and healing what was broken in him. Without a doubt there is power and energy in the touch of the human. Most men would swear on everything that the sweet loving touch of a woman for pain – specifically the pain of losing a child, a wife, a mother or homie, emotional pain – is probably the number one remedy. Support does come in many forms. Condolences from friends, a brother and other family members or even strangers. But when the emotional support names from a woman, a man is in love with there's nothing on the earth like it because love itself is so powerful. To Joker his losses are so devastating it feels like the end of the world. And then Uzenna… Tithi is there. This pure, innocent, Indian doctor girl who represents everything that's good. She gives him her body and then kisses him asleep. Tithi's touch is more powerful than she'll ever know.

CHAPTER SIX

Ghostman's Mansion
Wednesday 11:40 AM

First impressions are not everything because if they were Ghostman would have despised Valoria and her Mexican partners. Turns out these were not run-of-the-mill Mexican cartel members strictly focused on drug trafficking, warring with rivals or just killing politicians who got in their way. The Tijuana and Gulf cartels were now shifting their sights on the US stock market and retail businesses they could launder money through.

"Tattoo shops are not the most original idea," Nico was saying the following day over a delicious brunch meal. "But our Albanian friends are a very talented group. Valoria already has 200 former Albanian mafia members who are great tattoo artists."

Valoria cut to the chase. "The idea is to own tattoo shops around the country in or near drug-infested, gang-infested neighborhoods. The others we want to have situated in known party meccas like Miami – South Beach, Vegas, Houston, New York City, college towns, all through Meth Alley, Atlanta…"

"Basically," Honey B added on. "Wherever Red sets his sights, they also want to set up a tattoo shop."

"Hm." Ghostman was observing. Two hundred tattoo artists, he thought.

Valoria continued to explain. "His idea is to use off-book strip clubs to contract dealers, gangs, etcetera. Our idea is to use tattoo shops because what cop or fed you know gets a MS-13 tat… Or Gangster Disciple tat… Russian Mob or any other known gang ink on their body, face or neck?" She asked.

Now Ghost was starting to get it. "I think the idea is ingenious. Where's the little fuckin' boys and girls sex traffickin' come necessary? You're pokin' at a sleeping bear with that," Ghost warned.

"Is there not one American with cold blood anymore?" Valoria sighed. You want power and money… Or the glory and congratulations? You Americans are cry babies on the battlefields when a soldier falls. *No man left behind.*' In Albania it is an honor to die and let the animals and insects eat our flesh because, in the end, that's all we are. *Flesh.* We all eat from each other. I'm not in America to care about America law just take American money like they kill and take from everyone else."

Valoria paused for effect.

"Plus," Nico spoke up. "Joker Red is on borrowed time."

"Chittagong is a Bangladeshi city on the coast of the Bay of Bengal," Valoria stated. "One of the poorest villages you could imagine is there. Babies are sold for three sheep and one pig but it's enough meat to keep a family from starving. Men –and even some women – in England and America have a particular obsession with beautiful Bangladeshi girls, she explained.

"Fascinating women," Helena, who liked girls, admitted. "The blackest hair. Skin so pretty."

Valoria nodded and continued. "I have a rich client in Manchester, a wildly popular clothing designer, who pays fifty-thousand dollars for virgins as long as they are twelve to fourteen. He's a rigid man with cold bony fingers, so I can't imagine them falling in love with him. But I asked him: what's he to do with them? He says he 'tastes' them, and when he's bored with them, he sends them back to their country, rich."

"Dark web transactions?" Ghost asked.

"Mostly," Valoria nodded. "For the tattoo shops, I wouldn't supply Bangladeshi virgins. We would focus first on cream-of-the-crop Albanian teens looking to come to America to make some money. We will make them beautiful, tattoo their bodies, let them hang around the shops in scanty clothes, clean the shops, be cashiers. The Blood, Crips, Juggalos, Triads, Hells Angels, MS-13, Russian Mafia – whoever comes in and we recognize their tattoos get new gang tattoos… We put a girl on them."

"Take down their license plate," Honey B added. "Credit card information. We check them out through and through. Once they check out, we make offers of what they'll want. Coke, dope, weed, meth, weapons, encrypted cellphones, sex."

Now, Ghostman understood why the Mexicans were on board.

"Goddamn!" Ghostman explained. "Tattoos and investigator bitches on deck in the shop? I'm just picturin' myself as a sharp lil' crip or Mexican nigga from East L.A. with my shirt off being tatted while a bad white bitch is watchin' me and teasin' me. And she willing to give me head or some pussy? *At* the shop?"

Laughter around the room.

"Depending on location and space," Valoria told him. "We need health department certification so… say if we have a shop in a mall. You can't have sixteen-year-olds talking about it at school. We may strike a deal at the shop, but the deed will be done at our apartment building up the street. Make no doubt about it, the priority is the drugs and gun deals, but our girls will be there to fuck and suck for money, too, and we're talkin' a minimum of two hundred an hour."

Ghostman rubbed his hands together. "Joker Red's gonna find out and when he does it's best, he doesn't hear the words *sex traffickin'.* Especially of kids. How old will these tattoo girls be?"

"Their paperwork will say eighteen, nineteen, and twenty," Valoria said. "But since we're all partners… You know as far as I know that these girls will be fifteen, sixteen at *most.* The majority of them beggin' us to give them a better way. At twelve they were already whoring at the trainyards for food and coffee. At fifteen I didn't have to train them to fuck – they're *pornstars* in any man's bedroom by then. Albanian girls are loyal if treated right. And at least, they *look* eighteen, nineteen or twenty."

"What about health, V.D., AIDS…?" Ghost crossed his arms." Just throwin' out the variables."

"Before they leave, we have a doctor who checks them," Valoria explained. "We need money Honey B committed to because it makes us look legitimate. We can buy clothes, luggage, makeover for each girl, do hair, etcetera, before sending her to Mexico for fake modeling jobs. The Gulf organization will deliver them safely into the U.S. through Mexican and U.S. military connections. Let us handle the women," She urged him.

Honey B looked at him expectantly. "There are four organizations at this table: The Gulf Cartel, The Tijuana Cartel, The Albanian Mob, and us, Papi."

"NJË," Valoria corrected him.

"What's that again?" Ghost asked.

"N-J-Ë," Valoria spelled it out. "It means 'ONE' in my language."

"When will we meet the Moroccans and other Albanians you call this 'ONE'?" Ghostman inquired.

"Believe me," Valoria said slowly. "You never want the main One assassin to cross the seas. Bad enough, our army of two hundred tattoo artists will be here. For more than tattoos if needed."

It was a warning to everyone there.

CHAPTER SEVEN

Gates of Heaven Cemetery
Valhalla, New York
Sunday 2:30 PM

They were all memorialized at Gates of Heaven Cemetery in Valhalla, New York. Monk, Black N9NE, Eddie, Mustafa, Ground War, Julia, Melodie, Louise, Diane and Joker's four babies, had all been cremated and their ashes buried beneath the artsy marble headstones at the cemetery.

Everyone that had ever known the decedents were present for the sad occasion. Bible Reed had been chosen as the pastor over the memorial services and he did a splendid job. He gave an emotional, impassioned, inspirational, farewell to the fallen.

"Boss," Knarf whispered to Joker once it was over. "Skeeter's mom is here wantin' to talk to you… and Uzenna's tryna to get a minute."

"Son," Joker stated calmly but there was a coldness in his tone as well. "They both need to appreciate the air I'm letting them breathe," he scowled.

Knarf walked away.

Joker turned back to Don Frank and Vinnie Braga who were seated on chairs close to his. The ceremony was over.

"We have contracts with Chicago, Gary, Detroit and Milwaukee we want to let you in on," Frank said. "Medical waste disposal, waste disposal, road and bridge construction. President Biden just signed the Build Back Better Infrastructure Bill, and these cities are giving out *millions*."

"What the fuck can I do?" Joker had a lost look on his face. "I don't know shit about-."

"Whattaya mean you fuckin' goof?" Don Braga said. "We give you the lease on a downtown office in which you're the union delegate for our midwestern regional offices. Your office keeps fifteen precent, plus overhead and you deposit our money in our bank and that's that."

"I got so much shit I have to deal with right now," Joker sounded downtrodden, unsure. "The last thing I need is to fuck up a huge money venture with you. I appreciate the offer though."

"You *need* business to distract you," Don Braga wisely

advised. "I had a son who was murdered in Vegas. It nearly killed me."

"Then *my* son," Vinnie added.

"My nephew, Bobby," Don Braga nodded. "Within six months of each other. Bobby had just been made. My son wasn't a made guy, but enemies don't care when they want to hurt you. Trust me, the more you have to do the better."

"Call Leah," Joker told the mob bosses.

They sat looking at the row of headstones with sobering stares on their faces. Joker's lawyer, Mecca Montecristo stopped by crying, offering her condolences. Joker hugged her tightly and dried her eyes.

"Joker," she said sadly. "Who'd do this?"

"Some enemies choose to remain secret," He answered her as he looked down the hill and noticed two black Chevy Suburbans parked back-to-back on the service road. "But fortunately for me… I have others helpin' me uncover why and who would bomb half my whole family. Keep ya head up."

"David Joker Red Hodges!" Minnie snapped at him. "I've been tryna talk to you!"

O'Mira was nearby shaking her head.

"I'm dyin' of cancer and-"

He spun around, cutting her short. "Then die! With your rat bastard son!" He growled vehemently.

He left her standing there with her mouth open.

"You gonna get yours you cold blooded motherfucker!!" She screamed at his back

Bible was standing there.

"Whattayu lookin' at you ugly fuck?!" She breathed fire at him.

"You need Jesus," Bible told her. "I mean, you are about to meet him, ma'am," he pointed out.

But she stormed off. "Get out of my damned way!"

Joker reached the two suburban's and the rear passenger side window slid down. Nina Overstreet and Maxine Crawford sat inside. Driving was an unidentified black male in his mid to late 30s.

"There's a diner on Post Road about a mile north of here in Valhalla," Maxine said in that smoker's voice of hers." You got an ETA on when you'll wrap this up?"

"We're just millin' around," Joker told her. "What's this about?"

"We haven't spent months getting' set up for nothin'," Nina quipped.

He thought about Uzenna calling him a coward.

"The missions you mean," he said.

"Of course," Nina nodded affirmatively.

"Well," he stared at her. "We're warriors so I hope it's a lot of bullets involved."

"Easy, Blood hunter," Nina replied. "Plenty of time for killing. Post Road Diner. 20 minutes."

The windows closed and the two black suburban's pulled off. He looked back up the hill…

"Yeah," he said as he climbed into the back of a nearby Mercedes stretch limousine. "No better time like the present. Ayo, take me to Post Road Diner." The chauffeur nodded and drove away.

Ghostman, Bonecrusher, Knarf, Don Braga, and many other of his funeral guests looked on curiously as Joker's limousine sped away. But Knarf and Bible assured everyone that all was well, and that there would be a dinner party later at the Bonaventure Hotel in Larchmont.

"Wonder what that was about," Bonecrusher said to Knarf.

"Don't quote me," Knarf said. "But if I had to guess, it's mission time."

And Bonecrusher did exactly what Knarf said not to do and quoted him. As the funeral dispersed the number one thing on the EIE soldiers' minds was: Are we finally going on a mission?

The Post Road Diner
Valhalla, NY
Sunday 3:00 PM

CHAPTER EIGHT

The Post Road Diner

Valhalla, NY

Sunday 3:00 PM

Joker Red walked into the diner and his eyes immediately went to the far-left corner booth which was occupied by four people. One was the Department of Defense official Maxine Crawford and the other was Nina Overstreet. The other two – a man and a woman – were the drivers of the Chevy Suburbans and Joker wondered why they were here.

"These two ain't Uber drivers," Joker said as he sat down next to Nina.

"No, they're not," Nina replied. "They're FBI."

Joker sighed and tapped his fingers on the tabletop. "Hold on… Waitress!"

An older blond woman came over moments later. "May I take your order?"

"Bring a pot of coffee and a tray of assorted pastries," Joker instructed her. "And bring your boss over here, please?"

She did as he asked. Within a very short period of time a chubby, gray haired white man with a big nose came out wearing an apron with a broad smile on his face. "Hello!" He greeted the group.

Joker pulled out some cash folded inside of a golden and diamond Gucci money clip, saying. "We're gonna need you to close down the place while we're here… And also, for you and your waitress to disappear."

"I can't just…"

"Here's a thousand dollars," Joker handed him the cash. "Government business."

"Sure can." He took the money and locked the front door. Afterwards, he and his waitress ran into the rear door marked "Manager's Office" and disappeared.

Joker watched one of the two FBI agents, a black woman, pour everyone a cup of coffee. He waited for them to drink and then he followed.

"FBI," was all he said.

"CIA, by law, cannot act on domestic soil unless law enforcement attaches," Nina explained. "So, this is Special Agents Nyomi Malek and Brayson Bailey."

"Hm." Joker shook his head. "What did I tell y'all? Each

time we meet it's more and more government."

"Just covering our ass," Maxine said.

"We might as well fly down to the Pentagon right now and meet with SOCOM (Special Operations Command) or the JSOTF (Joint Special Operations Task Force)," he stated.

Maxine and Nina chose not to reply to his sarcasm. They knew about his tragic losses and didn't see any need to stoke the fires.

"We are not overlooking anyone or anything in the hunt for the bomber or bombers of your loved ones," Nina assured him. "We swear to that."

He nodded and sipped his coffee. "I appreciate that… It means a lot. But y'all know nothing so far?"

"Not yet," Nina stated. "These types of analyses take time."

"Aight," he shrugged. "So… why y'all here?"

"Marcellus Xanaphoulous," Nina should showed him a picture of a man with dark brown hair and eyebrows so thick they looked fake.

"Zanaffa-what?" Joker took the cell phone she held and examined the photo more closely. "He doesn't look familiar."

"X-A-N-A-P-H-O-U-L-O-U-S," Nina spelled it out. "'Zanaffalos.'"

"A Greek?" Joker asked.

"Close but not close enough," Nina said. "Keep swiping the screen to the left."

He followed directions. *"Serbian. 'From Subotica — a city at the northernmost tip of Serbia where his army trains and continues to grow bolder. They are using their influence in the tracking and railroad industry to run sex slaves From Chernivtsi, Ukraine, back into Serbia and into Albania. The Ukrainian women are refugees fleeing war between Russia and Ukraine.' What we have uncovered is not just women being lured into the lucrative Dark Net Pornography market, but most are underage, etcetera, etcetera."*

He calmly flipped through dozens of images the FBI/CIA had "come across" via the Dark Net.

#1. A young girl, in the 4th or 5th Grade at best, was handcuffed from behind, dressed in a French maids uniform. A man, about 45 to 50 years old, seated in a cushioned chair while the elementary school girl fellated him as if she'd been doing it for years.

"She's been doing this for a while," Joker whispered loud enough for the others to hear, "She's not visibly upset ... or she could be doped up..."

"Yeah," Nina nodded. "This is someone's baby girl."

#2. A woman, about 20 years old or so, was in a video tied down across the end of a sofa with her white bottom bare, her vagina and anus visible. She had been whipped so brutally that blood was dripping from the wounds. Her mouth was duct taped, tears were pouring from her eyes and a large sex toy was being shoved into her as she tried to scream.

"Clearly a sexual-torture video," Nina described it. "I watched it and learned that it had over four million encrypted viewers worldwide. Multiply that by ten to twenty- five cents per viewer and imagine the weapons these bastards have with that kind of cash."

"And how much of that cash buys Afghan heroin," Maxine added. "And what the Taliban is doing with that cash. You see how they beat Trump, Biden and America's ass in recently and kicked us out of their country."

#3. A girl who looked to be no older than 12 held two babies in her arms. One of the

Babies was breastfeeding while the older one slept. The girl was clearly nude and appeared to be depressed and underfed.

"This one says it all, huh?" Nina asked Joker who seemed to be stuck on that one photo. "She's twelve, maybe thirteen, with two babies she's still nursing. No woman I ever met was still nursing the first baby while she had the next one."

"Okay," Joker nodded. "Where's this piece of shit?"

"Interpol tracked him to the United States," Nina told him. "However,… there's so much more story here."

Joker stared at her. "Well, what fuckin' story?"

"There won't be any arrest in the case," Nina said. "You need to understand this going in."

Joker really stared at her now.

"No arrest, no extradition," Nina added more slowly this time." Not For Marcellus or any of his gunmen."

No arrest, no extradition only meant one thing.

The shit just got more interesting.

"Aha," Joker muttered, staring at a photo of Xanaphoulous. "So there will be a lot bullets."

CHAPTER NINE

Mecca Montecristo & Red
Madison Avenue, Manhattan

There were certain lines that Joker drew for himself in the sand to be better able to control himself because he knew who he was. And that imaginary line acted as a reminder that he'd put it there not only because he knew Joker Red but to also protect those he valued very highly. One of those he valued very highly was the tall, rich and brilliant star attorney Mecca Montecristo. He knew that Meca had a Madison Avenue apartment that had likely cost millions to obtain due to it overlooking Central Park. She had rich neighbors and about a fourth of them were celebrities like Kelly Ripa, one of the Bush daughters, Diddy, Jennifer Lopez and others.

He was cleared through the doorman and then the security desk in the lobby prior to him getting on the elevator and riding it up to her floor. He rang the doorbell, and she opened it within seconds. As soon as she stepped aside to let him into her opulent New York City apartment he was sure of himself and he felt good that he'd come.

Power and Beauty. She personified it. Her home reflected what and who she was. She was one of those women with skin so flawless and hair so long, black, and clean that she looked fresh out of the shower and a high-end beauty salon. She always looked like she was well put together.

"You gonna be okay?" she asked him in a small voice. They were standing in the foyer at first. He nodded.

She walked up to him and removed his trendy brim and the expensive black Armani overcoat. She hung them on the shiny brass railing of the staircase. Her apartment was two levels. She lived alone except for a juvenile macaw and her tropical fish.

"I'm… lost I guess." He shrugged. Following her halfway to the immaculate living room. She stopped and stood with her back up against the wall of the hallway. She walked up to him, grabbed his left hand. "I ain't come to stress you out or nothin'. I'm just still in town and …"

"You're not," she assured him, taking him into her living room and calling out, "Alexa! Play my R&B Smooth Tunes Playlist."

The robotic voice replied by playing soft music in the

background beginning with a song by Trey Songz. He watched the 5 feet 10-inch-tall high-powered attorney saunter sensually across the wide expansive living room. She wore beige silky gym shorts which she liked to sleep in along with a black T-shirt and pink ankle socks. She knew that his eyes were following her as she went behind the bar and made them both drinks.

"This place is really nice," he complimented her as she handed him a double of Hennessy. When she did his fingers touched hers and they lingered there, Her glance caught his while they touched.

"You wanna sit-?" she said.

"You wanna sit-?" he said in chorus with her, and they laughed. "Hey, I don't know why I pulled up… I'm lyin'. I always be wantin' to check up on you but…"

"Go ahead," she urged him in that lovely Italian-English accent of hers. "David 'Joker Red' Hodges. Don't go getting' shy."

"I'm not I've always wanted to respect your space," he told her.

She looked around the luxuriously furnished living room, indicating with a hand gesture. "I never thought in a million years of reaching where I am before the age of fifty. You're my most generous client. What space are you?"

"I like you," he blurted out.

Now she was the shy one. But she quickly closed her mouth, drained her drink, and looked at him. "I know," out came her answer. "I think I like you, too."

"I always have," he declared as she rose onto her feet and

walked back behind the fully stocked bar. But he was on her heels as she grabbed the tequila and poured herself a double.

When he looked at the 34-year-old, borderline light skinned woman, he saw R&B pop superstar *IRENE CARA* and *BAE DAWN CHONG* in one sexy crossover – when they were 21. Her Nigerian father was a very handsome man and Caterina Montecristo had been a model in her hometown which was Milan, Italy.

"You're so beautiful," he whispered as he looked at her in the mirror behind the bar. She stared at the ruthless criminal mastermind, feeling the massive bone as it grew hard against her.

She turned around and after looking into his eyes, gave him one of the most heartwarming and heartbreaking smiles he'd ever seen. *"Heartbreaking"* only because of how pretty she was. He caught her lovely mouth with his own and wrapped her slender body up inside of his big, long, arms. Behind strength and electricity which had her toes curling up, her nipples turning harder than nickels, and she could feel her anal and pussy muscles clenching as though they were commanded by a nurse to make a fist for a blood drawing.

They moaned and whined into each other's mouth. That's when he heard her scream, shake and bite into his neck and shoulder as his left hand went down into her pussy and his right found the smooth dark cleft of her buttocks and his middle finger lovingly circled her anus. The pleasure was way too much! She pushed away from him.

"Joker, my god!" She stepped away from him, shaking her head but he stopped her in her tracks.

"Uhn Uhn, where da fuck you think you goin'?" He hissed, flushed up against her soft ear, nipping at it and her neck. He picked her up and walked with her over to the sofa and removed her top, revealing her gorgeous c-cup breasts.

Almost immediately he was suckling those perfectly rounded beauties. He laid her down, and the high-powered lawyer reached to pull him down so that he would keep sucking on her and biting her delicious-tasting nipples. He noticed that her areolae were not large like a lot of other women who had silver dollar-sized areolas. Mecca's areolas were more like quarters.

"Don't stop suckin' 'em," her voice cracked.

He stopped to strip naked for her first. "You ain't got no man around, do you?"

"They're intimidated," she breathed, unable to keep her eyes away from his manhood and the rest of his beautiful body. He looked jacked and what he had hangin' between his legs she just dared not describing it at all.

He couldn't resist her sweet breasts. Their caramel-n-honey color, their size and shape, and how her dark nipples stiffened and sat upward, begging to be kissed. He did so much more than that and she really loved it.

"I'm not intimidated," he stated while biting those gorgeous nipples, kissing each goose egg-sized orb and slowly swirling his long tongue around it, He reached underneath her, and she lifted her ass up so he could take her off her shorts.

"I can see you're not intimidated," she said.

He left her shorts on. "I was about to eat dat pussy, make

that clit crazy…tongue fuck ya ass. But hell nah. I see you lookin' at this monster dick."

"Mm hm. So?" She was actually staring at it. How huge the balls were.

"*So?*" he mimicked her. "This is how its gonna go. Before I do all the wonderful lusty things, I have in mind to do to you I wantchu on your knees kissin' an' lickin' and suckin' me. Swallow the first one and show me whatchu got."

As a woman who was used to telling everyone else around her what to do for her, this sure was a change-up. If it had been anyone else, she would've fired them or told them to kiss her ass. But Joker knew her well. It actually turned her on something fierce to have the tables turned and be told what to do. Especially in an area where she actually was not an expert. She was not a virgin, but she also lacked sexual experience. She's had very few men, she wasn't interested in women and the few men she'd had been intimate with had let her be the dominant one in the relationship and the bed. With Joker, she was willing to do anything for him. She'd always been attracted to him.

She nodded and reached for his quadriceps which she held onto as she slid down off the sofa to the carpeted floor. She was so horny that she began moaning even before his big warm penis had touched her lips. She'd sucked dick before but nothing this long or so thick. He saw her eyes close when she held him by the base with one hand and by the balls with the other. He knew in that few seconds her eyes were closed that she was taking in his scent. She couldn't even fit him in her mouth at first.

"Hey, hey – c'mere, honey," he said pulling her face forward.

"It's so big," she laughed.

He kissed her watering mouth. "Just kiss, lick, keep on, lickin' it all the way around. Then. Don't be shy, Ain't no judge, D.A., jury no cameras watchin'. No rich bitch lawyer needin' to bed perfect. You ever spit on da sidewalk?"

She shook her head. "No."

"Spit on my dick," he instructed her. "In here, you my dick suckin' cum slut. Repeat it."

"I'm your dick suckin' cum slut," she told him shyly.

"Is your pussy wet?"

"Oh my god yes," she answered insanely horny.

He took off her shorts, and also the thong panties. He put her back on her knees and smelled the panties and the shorts. "Ever since we first met, I wondered what your pussy smells like, if you had hair in your asscrack-do you?"

She blushed under his bold questioning. "I'm not...I don't...I mean... No."

"You don't know," he stated. She shook her head. "Do you know what your cunt smells like?"

"Like honey dew melon," she replied. He let her smell the panties. "I love how my cunt smells. Do you?"

"I *adore* how it smells. Lick all around the head...kiss it... suck the head in and out...spit on it...make it slick and slippery," he coached her after she began to work on his gigantic fuck stick.

This time she relaxed and got way more into it. She licked up and down on that beautiful cock all the while her pussy was tingling with passion and leaking her love cream all down the soft insides of her thighs. Pretty soon she was clutching that giant cucumber in her left hand while stroking the slickened baton up against her left cheek. Her saliva mixed with his pre-ejaculate had him drenched everywhere. She licked and sucked his balls, mesmerized by how big he was. She loved how clean-shaven he was, He was so smooth and well-groomed that her tongue craved more and more of him. What was weird was how hard his balls were and she swore, that she could feel his heart beating through that huge cock of his.

"Go, baby, shit yeah, fuck!" he cursed as she wormed her fingers all over his lubed-up scrotum then found his anus. She faced-fucked him while finger swirling the inner ring of his asshole. Up and down, in and out it went…

The glans of his great pulsating cock grew then spurted multiple globs of hot semen into Mecca's hungry mouth. At the first taste she started moaning…then he could actually hear her as she swallowed down as much cum as she could. She continued to lick his salty-sweet dick until it was all gone except for the cum that had dribbled down her chin, neck, and throat.

"It's still hard," she finally said. She licked her chin, swiping her tongue to the left and right.

He nodded as she rose and pulled him with her to her bedroom. "You say that like you're surprised, Mecca."

"Well…anybody else cum like that they'd be balled up like a baby asleep," she said as they entered her bedroom. It was decorated in all-white and was as immaculately maintained as the rest of the apartment.

"I'm not anybody else," he declared as she went to use the bathroom.

When she emerged her hair was brushed out in waves that fell past her shoulders. She climbed onto the queen-sized bed where he was seated on the side of it. He turned to her and almost immediately they were in a sensuous, mad wet, lip-lock. At first, she thought it would be a moment that he'd kiss her…and then maybe a moment more…but it turned out to be so much more. Joker Red was giving Mecca Montecristo his lips, his body, his most sensual foreplay possible and she was caught up in his lovemaking.

Joker loved her gorgeous breasts, and she loved even more the way he squeezed on them, sucked on them and pinched her nipples. Any man would fall in love with her over her breasts alone. They were too pretty not to. While looking at her droplets of sweat and his saliva as he licked and sucked them caused him to finger her pussy and smear her cunt cream all over her nipples.

"My god that's so sexy!" she gasped as he smelled her breasts and suckled on them until the cunt scent disappeared. She looked at how big and hard his dick got as he did that. "Fuck me with it, Joker."

But instead, Joker put her onto her belly and spread her legs. While continuing to squeeze her titties he laid down and started to suck on her clit, labia, pussyhole, and her entire butt slice. His tongue didn't only crave dipping in and out of her honey holes, but her entire slice was tasty. She was out of her mind with what Joker was doing to her.

The beautifully Black lawyer bounced that ass and pussy up and down on the mattress, pushing her sweet orifices into and out of Joker's eager mouth and nose. She sobbed with lust as he went to town on her. As she came down form her third orgasm, she realized that he was on top of her back, his mammoth man-piece was kissing the drippy lips of her labia...then, the knobby head plopped inside of her front entrance.

"Joker, please!" She whined and froze up afraid of taking any more.

"You okay, beautiful lady?" he asked her suddenly.

"I'm not used to it," she admitted and even mentioned that she could barely recall her last time. "It hurts."

"I gotchu," he assured her. All the while he was busy licking away all the salty-sweet droplets of her perspiration form the back of her neck and shoulders. He pressed and slowly pushed in and out of her tight pussy until he was buried deep. "Got-damn you tight, baby!"

In a few short minutes almost the only thing that could be heard was the slap! slap! slap! slap! Sounds of his sweaty skin smacking her ass and the moans, groans and other sounds of sex. He knew he was pounding up against her G-spot and proof of it came five minutes later when she yelped and wailed out another one of her hot, sexy orgasms. When Mecca exploded, she wailed and he just knew it was, because it was a reaction very different from the others.

Afterward, he turned her over and slid back inside of his

prominent attorney. She was turnt all the way up now, so he pumped into her sloppy wet pussy very slowly. Then he began to fuck her harder and harder. As his steel-hard pole slipped in and out of the Class-A female, she wrapped her long legs around his waist and started fucking him back. So, they were slamming into each other extremely hard. His big, heavy balls were bouncing against her ass as he banged her hard and deep. Neither of them kept track of how long they went at it but after some time of his really hard fucking he slammed into her steaming hot pussy and burst into a million starts as the semen gushed wetly inside of her. The way she screamed and wailed made him believe that the police would be showing up.

She looked down at where their genitals were connected, and she saw milky white sperm bubbles. They kissed and held each other tightly, doing their best to catch their breath. They fell into a peaceful slumber before starting back up on each other again.

CHAPTER TEN

The Ethnicity Dance Company
Chicago, IL

Eliminating the Chicago streets of menacing cartel crew members and henchmen - - via the infamous 80-man Hit List – had opened big doors for EIE crystal meth. Chicago was the *Key*, the so-called heartbeat of the EIE brand being established not just in Chicago but all throughout the Midwest. Particularly, in what has become known as "Meth Alley:" Nebraska, Kansas, Iowa, Missouri, Illinois, Indiana, and Kentucky.

Joker knew that once those states were under his dominant control the rest of the world would fall in line. Including the Dark Net which had very few borders or limits to where the meth could be shipped.

Needless to say, by the coming Winter, the entire Meth Alley will be under his lock and key. And Joker gives credit where credit is due. It was a team effort: the mighty muscle of his army, Meth Man Ace's chemical ingenuity, Don Braga's mastermind and political clout, and one other thing.

The strippers.

Them bitches is beasts. They work with no clothes on, no guns, no Kevlar vests. They dance, do acrobatic tricks, pole dancing, bussin' open all that pussy, making them titties shake, and making them tattooed asses clap all night till the sun comes up. They recognize all the hustlers and spread word about moving meth. Even if a Latin King, Gangster Disciple, or MS-13, never even sold meth these bitches talked them into it either after a lap dance, some head, or hot steamy sex. The girls would literally give them a crash course in meth dealing and show the dealers how much money they were losing if they didn't have the cheap drug in their inventory.

One thing about five energetic young women – especially money hungry strippers - - that young ass could be displayed anywhere on earth and men – and women – would come out to see it, touch it, kiss it, lick it and stick it. From the business districts across middle America, through every White, Latino or Black ghetto in the Hoods, to every suburban area, and even high up in the rural hills and mountains, or low-lying backwood regions and swamplands along the southern states.

At first the strippers seemed to be coming on board slowly. Honey B and the other core EIE strippers had to poach them from other clubs. But Instagram, Snapchat, Twitter and Facebook were real. *Especially* Instagram! Every bad ass ghetto chick in America is on Instagram, looking for a way to come up.

All of the core EIE strippers made videos and commercials putting out a national call to all strippers. Honey B, Destinee, Carla Deleon, Jessika Cicero, Isabella Caronna, Yolie Santana, Crystal, Pollyanna, Avi, Mika, Olivia, Lady, Kitten, Sinnamon, Yadi Molina, Tiera, Jayda, Tiffani and Journee all got involved and stuck to the same narrative:

"IF YOU A BAD YOUNG BITCH TRYNA HUSTLE FOR THAT HUMMER, nice crib, Prada and Tiffanys money then y'all need to come to Chicago and start getting it day one. Ain't nobody got time for games or gimmicks. Just get here and we got you. Hotel, food, transportation, all that. Now, if you ugly, too fat, ain't got no dancin' skills stay yo ass home! But if you still bad as shit and can't dance, we can work with that. 18 to 25 only. However, 14 to 17 can come if you have parental consent. Come straight to EIE Ethnicity Dance Company in Chicago. Show up any time, open 24-7."

LITERALLY, DOZENS OF PROFESSIONAL COMMERCIALS/VIDEOS were produced, and mass distributed on all the major social media advertising forums. And from there it took off. Though Joker had had Leah and Uzenna register the EDC as an actual dance studio it was anything but. It was actually a recently closed down fitness center/gymnasium that was thoroughly cleaned up and outfitted with comfortable bunk beds and lockers for the flocks of strippers coming into town.

Ten, twenty, thirty, forty, fifty, sixty … one hundred, two hundred, three hundred and the numbers kept rising. Pretty girls, curvy girls, White, Black, Latina, Asian, Brazilian, Bolivian, some didn't even speak English, many lied about their ages but if they looked good, they were allowed to stay!

EDC had two stories, large group shower areas, saunas, jacuzzis, but they were running out of bed space. On top of that every time they looked up there was another underage girl showing up with a fake parental consent letter. Joker had a strict policy of not allowing minors to stay at the gym. They were sent to the Twin Towers.

"How old are you?" Joker had asked one such teenager. She was tall, skinny and lanky with sandy blond hair and crystal blue eyes. "Don't lie to me either. I'm not gonna call the cops or send you back home."

"I'm fourteen but I'm a woman," she'd told him.

"Analise Shoemaker is your real name?"

She nodded.

"Why are you a runaway?"

"My mom's a drunk and my dad's in prison for life," she'd admitted. "My mom beats me because all her boyfriend's hit on me…"

"You a virgin?"

She'd hesitated. "No, why? You want me to suck your cock or let you fuck me?"

"Yeah," he'd said. "When you stop wearin' a trainin' bra," he kidded around with her. "I'm not a pedophile, slim."

She laughed. "I'm not a virgin. One of my mom's boyfriends helped me with that when I was twelve. But I do have a very pretty pussy."

"You *look* young, innocent and fresh," he told her. "Ima show you how to make money without havin' to give away the most precious part of you I don't want it, baby doll."

First it was Annalise (14, White); Katalina Gambino (15, White); Kayla Guido (15, white); Martinique "Lolo" Parker (14, Black) Michelle Torre (16, White); Lyssandra Bazzi (l6, white); and Remy Browning (15, Black). Any underage girls that came to EDC that Joker knew about he would put under his own special protection. They were way too vulnerable not to.

When Ghostman demanded why, Joker was a bit annoyed. "Because they need a *real* Daddy. They world is full of predators, and they need protection … from boogeymen like you, huh?"

"Save-A-Hoe ass nigga," Ghostman had called him.

Joker knew that pretty females attracted a lot of the wrong attention. But beautiful underaged girls were a whole 'nother product indeed. They attracted monsters. He'd called Don Braga who owned a dozen of Chicago's hottest bars.

"Don Braga," Joker had said to him.

"J.R!" The Don boomed.

"I have seven minors – all females," Joker had begun. "If I'm a guy out drinkin' or passin' by your club and see the sweet face of these young women I'm goin' in! They are fuckin' magnets."

"You mean 'bait girls', right?" The Don said right away. "Uh oh. How young?"

"Fourteen to sixteen – seven of 'em." Joker had answered. "They're street vet's already, they know how to handle men, how to flirt, etcetera. But I don't want them sellin' sex. Let's show 'em somethin' different."

The minors were kept away from the meth, the underground strip club scene and all the other "big boy" shit, much to Honey B and Ghostman's dismay. But the real boss was Joker Red. And though he had taken his eyes off of the stripper plan at first, he had quickly woken up, established EDC, and then he let Honey B and Ghostman expand the meth brand throughout Meth Alley. That expansion meant opening up new underground strip clubs in each of the seven Meth Alley states and supplying each club with at least ten girls.

Nevertheless, the plan took off like a NASCAR race but Joker had no idea about the treachery being cooked up behind his back with his own underboss's knowledge. Betrayal like this is as grimey as it's ever going to get.

CHAPTER ELEVEN

Green Point, Brooklyn
Sunday 8:00 PM

Joker used the Nissan Pathfinder he had stolen to disguise himself. First, he applied make-up to darken his skin. Then he put on false eyelashes, to make his own appear thicker. He popped brown contacts into his eyes to conceal his own green ones. He wore a wig made out of shortened dreadlocks with tinges of brownish red in them.

He took all of 45 minutes to fully prepare his face, hair, and clothes. When he was ready, he drove out of the White Castle Restaurant parking lot and headed up to Graham Avenue in the Green Point section of Brooklyn.

NYPD Detective Hanna Genovese was the niece of notorious Chicago crime boss Frank Braga. And she had been working on the inside of the NYPD for her uncle for nearly a decade. And since Don Braga and Joker had joined forces, Joker had Inherited the same benefits that the Don enjoyed in knowing her.

However, the relationship that Hanna had with her uncle's New York crime partners was extremely strained and had been deteriorating all the last year. As much as Don Braga loved his sister Margie … he could not take a chance with her daughter's being taken down by the New York Police Department's Internal Affairs Division.

And from what he'd heard they were moving in on her fast. And, unbeknownst to her, so was Joker Red.

9:30 PM

He picked up her trail when she left her Graham Avenue apartment building at 9:30 PM and climbed inside of her new Mercedes SUV. According to the surveillance Don Braga's spies had done on her she usually stopped for gas and coffee on her way to work at the Exxon Gas / Mini Market on Greenpoint Avenue, about six blocks east from her home.

When she pulled into the station Joker waited for her to walk into the market, grab her coffee, pay for her gas and return to the pump. However, she didn't pay for the gas inside of the market. She only purchased cigarettes and coffee and then paid for her fill-up at the pump with a credit card.

He made his move.

He stepped out of his vehicle and without a moment's hesitation used a silenced M9 Beretta to rob her.

"Purse!!!" he hissed. "Make a Funny move I'll kill you!!"

She quickly handed him her Hermès bag. "I know you…"

That was as far as she got.

PPPHHHFFFTTT!! PPPHHHFFFTT!!!

One to the face, the other to the neck. Then just as quickly as it had all started it was over.

There were eyewitnesses to the robbery and the shooting. There were also surveillance cameras. By the time the police had a description of the getaway vehicle and its driver, both were ghosts. Joker later gas-soaked the car, his clothes, shoes and wig with it inside of his own warehouse in Otisville. A slow, controlled burn.

The next day, he had the pile of burnt scrap hauled off to the junkyard where it was smashed and melted down into nothing along with the gun.

That should've been that, but it wasn't. He had other unfinished business to take care of in New York. He thought long and hard about everything.

It don't matter how much money a nigga make how big the fuckin' mansions, cars, airplanes or no matter the number of bad bitches I get to fuck, own, and put babies in … I'm still from the mufuckin' streets. I ain't lettin' go of no form of betrayal! I don't give a fuck who it is!

So he took it back to the streets.

With bullets. Lots of bullets.

JOKER WAS ESCORTED INTO MECCA'S OFFICE AT THE END OF THE hall by a Black female legal secretary. Mecca waved him in as she concluded a telephone call. "Hello, Red," she greeted him.

He looked around the enormous office. "Nice. Real nice."

She came out from behind the desk and hugged him as he hugged her. It was close, warm, cozy, sensual and loving.

"You like my present?" he asked her with a smile and several kisses.

She pointed at the desk. "The Spanish Vargueño. It's Sixteenth Century. I love it. It was history. Thank you. What's up with you?

"How do you feel?" he asked her. "Honestly. About us."

"You've brought me out of my shell," she state as they sat down on the black leather sofa. "But I know you're polyamorous. You have a dozen women…perhaps more. I know you love them. I had doubts of how one man could sexually please so many women and I literally can see how. You're physically capable-no doubt. You're so big that a woman needs a couple days to heal from one night with you."

"We gon' be cool? You ain't gonna be jealous or nothin'?"

"Never jealous and never a lesbian." She was firm on that

point. "My door's open. So, whenever you're ready-come home."

That was huge peace of mind for the Brooklyn gangster.

CHAPTER TWELVE

The Ghostman Mansion
Monday Evening

"Mission? What mission?" Honey B inquired of Ghostman as they relaxed in the outdoor Jacuzzi at their Winthrop Harbor Estate.

"Top secret right now," Ghostman told her. "You know we have to fulfill periodic contract work for the Department of Defense from time to time and can't say no."

"This is just perfect," Honey B frowned. "We have all this work we have to do with the tattoo shops, moving these girls around … it's fucked up timin'."

"Well, if you can't handle it… "Ghost chose his words carefully. "Simply stall Valoria out until I return."

"Of course, I can handle it. I just don't want to be stuck explain why you ain't around when she knows I answer to you. That's why I told you how important it was that I appear to be the boss."

"Do whatever you need to," he told her. "While we was up New York the nigga was totally distracted but the big brass showed up and obviously they handed down some mission work we gotta do. I was tryna gauge whether he found out anything about the hits…"

"Nothin'?"

"Crickets. Don Braga, DOD, CIA – I got nothin'."

"Don't panic."

"I'm frosty," he said as he picked her up and carried her out of the Jacuzzi. "You lookin' crazy hot with your belly showin' right now."

"Cuidado, Papi, I'm delicate," she said and kissed him. "I'm horny too but let me sixty-nine you and then ride it so I control how much goes in."

"You hurtin' down there?"

She shook her head. "Just nervous cause of the baby. You feel ten fuckin times bigger deep inside. So don't touch all the way or we can miscarriage."

"I got you sweet little Mami…"

TUESDAY MORNING

The following day, Honey B drove the canary Lamborghini Gallardo into Chicago and parked in her reserved parking space behind the Ethnicity Dance Company. Although it was only 9:30 AM the women were up and at it: some working out, others in the swimming pool, saunas, or Jacuzzis, a few more on cellphones or laptops, some smoking —

"What?!" Honey B scolded a group of young Black women. "Uhn-uh! Ain't no smokin' in this buildin'! Y'all bitches should know better! And y'all need to mask up, too! C'mon now!"

Honey B walked through the lower-level bunk bed area and straight to the manager's office. She got on the loud speaker and made a brief announcement:

"Everyone gather inside of the second-floor gym area. Got great news. Everybody."

She went upstairs, making sure she had on her N-95 face mask due to the rise in Omicron infections inside of the city.

She looked around and said: "I love looking at you fine ass *chicas*! So many of y'all right now."

Which was true. They lined up in pre-planned rows: Black girls, White girls and Latina or Mixed girls:

DAZIA MOORE
    Cinni Bee
    Mercedes
    Lidia Goban
    Kennedy
    Dominique
    Dara

Jayla
Shantel Renee
Domineek "LaLa" Martin
Strella
Tyler Ward
Shana
Gizelle
Dina Dior
Teresa
Roxanne
Jhonni
Gemini
Mya Fiya
Mahogani
Sara May
Tamara
Mynx
Natalee Love
Pinkki
Kendra
Trinidad Jane
Chayanne
Josi
Abigail (Abby)
Aryanna Jacobs
Sahara Heat
Lovely "The Real Goddess"
Mimi Amore
Lena

CeCe

Lia Cheeks

Yazzy (Yasmine)

Zmeena

Wet Rayne

Bree

Porsha Caprice

Mikayla

Alia

Chela

Irene May

Nina

Tay

Sasha

Kiara

Brianna Raven

Sommer

Joseline

Lorraine

Katavia

Lelah

Staci

Scarlett

Gia

Mare Zimora

Chelsey

Egypt

Taylor Love

Valentina

Pumpkin

Jenna Jay

Adia Monteleone

Lacie Elliot

Frenchy Kisses

Ava De Luca

Elba Free

Stephy Ragusa

Keisha "Kakes" Narducci

Star

Amber

Candice "Sparkles" Gazians

Duchess

Lindsay

Nicole "Nenny" Snow

Gwendolyn

Nikita

Corinne Falcone

Alycia

Eva "Lynx" Cannavale

Susy "Sweets" Ciccone

Jayonna

Nadia Baratta

Kagney Tabrizi

Allenna

Shaina

Kelsie Sollito

Solea

Savannah "Goldie" Cevicchi

Gia Fiore
Loni
Ruby Giuletta
Cali Bottari
Cameo
Priscilla Delgotto
Hailee Cobirossi
Anastasia Palladino
Abella
White Girls:
Laina
Anikka Torelli
Penny Lee
Sukie
Kissa Rae
Julianna Blair
Violet
Sweet Venus
Lacey Foxx
Gabriella Machione
Lisa Lips
Rozie
Bella DeValerio
Jazzie
Amanda
Ayanna Lullo
Skylar
Christine
Tori St. James

Harley Monroe
Jezabell Bond
Ariana
Jennifer Stratton
Romera
Mariah
Lexie
Audrey Blake (twins)
Aubry Blake (twins)
Samia
Cassandra (Cassidy)
Kayla
Alexis
Bridgette
Piggy (Latina/ Black)
Vicki
Flora Alvarez
Kassidi Kream
Octavia Luna
Elle
Zoe
Riley
Aja Costello
Mazerati
Holly "The Body"
Racquel
Aphrodite Bosworth
Ariella Scalese
Latinas/Mixed Girls:

Apolina Noriega

Kesha

Canela

Sophia

Carmen

Diamand

Marta

"Mm!" Honey B smiled, looking around lustfully as she waited for a count. "All bad bitches!"

Dazia walked up to her.

"How many we got, Dazia?" Honey B asked the General Manager of the EDC, a beautiful Black girl with peanut butter brown skin and light brown eyes.

"Um, one hundred and sixty," the curvy little Dazia stated, reading from a clipboard. "All of you get ready to ship out," she said loud enough for everyone to hear her. "We have new people comin' in so pack up, leave it clean and come get your plane ticket or train ticket... or in a few cases your Uber driver's info."

"That wasn't long," the sexy Latina dancer Apolina said. "Where we goin'?"

"Look at your ticket Mija," Honey B told her noticing how cute she looked in white boy shorts that showed off the exact outline of her puffy young pussylips. "As a matter of fact, c'mere."

Apolina was 5'2", had long shiny hair she kept in one long Pocahontas braid, she was tattooed head to toe it seemed. Honey B knew she was Panamanian from the Flag tatted on her neck. She had brown eyes, lovely teeth and skin the color of creamy coffee.

"Hm?" Apolina stopped in front of Honey.

"You *tryna* leave today?" Honey asked her.

Apolina nodded. "I never been around so many catty females."

"That's not what I asked." Honey B made it obvious what she meant by staring at the young beauty's pierced belly button and in between her legs.

"Ohhh," Apolina blushed. "You mean ... hang with *you*? I'm so silly."

Honey nodded. "Yeah, I mean…"

Apolina hesitated. "I'm not gonna lose the position? Because I have credit card bills, cellphone, and-"

"Girl," Honey shushed her. "You got a cash app?"

"Duh, who doesn't?"

"Tell it to me. Honey B used the app on her phone to access her own cash app and within two minutes she sent a transfer of $1000 to Apolina's cash app.

"Oh, okay!" Apolina squealed when she received the digital notification. "A thousand dollars!"

"Go get your things, chica," Honey B told her. "Your hot little ass is rollin' wit me."

As for the rest of the girls, they were being sent to all 48 of the underground strip clubs opened throughout Meth Alley. None of them could be used in the plan to backdoor Joker Red with the tattoo shops that were being opened as all of this regular EIE business was going on. Each club was already staffed with private mercenary security and at least fifteen strippers each but it didn't matter. The more the merrier.

Honey B hoped like hell the tattoo shops could catch up and keep up with the massive underground empire Joker had built. He now had close to a thousand women going hard for him in the bootleg stripper circuit. The women absolutely loved the clubs they were at because they drank all the alcohol they wanted, kept the tips for themselves, they picked and choose who they wanted to have sex with and they kept 100% of the money they were paid for it. The girls also received large cash bonuses, and gifts such as cars, clothes, jewelry and other luxuries for moving meth.

Honey B wasn't sure but she "guesstimated" that EIE/Joker was pulling down somewhere in the neighborhood of in $10-$20M per month. The DOD/CIA knew it, the Chicago Crime Syndicate knew it, Honey B knew it and now the Albanians and Mexicans knew it.

To move in on a blood hunter like Joker the plan had to be foolproof. If not, there was going to be blood everywhere.

CHAPTER THIRTEEN

Ghostman's Mansion
Tuesday Night

Apolina Noriega was not gay but every now and then a woman would come along that brought the "closet lesbian" out of her. Right now, as she followed Honey B into the Winthrop Harbor mansion, Apolina was seriously checking her out.

"How many months are you?" Apolina asked.

"Why?" Honey replied with a question "You too nervous to touch me?"

"Actually…" Apolina hesitated. "It makes you look sexier. I'm hopin' I know what to do."

Honey got her inside of the Foyer and kissed her mouth,

very slowly at first, slipping her tongue deeply inside. Honey loved straight women so much because they were so shy at first.

"You taste like cinnamon," Honey B said, pulling the Panamanian goddess by the hand up the winding staircase. "Apolina what? Is Apolina your real name?"

"Apolina Dulce Marín Noriega," she properly introduced herself. "I'm nineteen, from Miami, but Panamanian."

Honey B undressed and Apolina actually loved what she saw. "I'm so fuckin' horny," Honey B admitted.

She scooted up on the bed, spreading her legs wide showing Apolina her bald pussy, shiny and wet from the juices leaking out of her. She palmed her breasts and pinched her nipples as Apolina stared. The cute Panamanian girl undressed and continued to watch Honey put on a show, pleasing herself. Honey B had a very pretty pussy as well.

"You have such a beautiful body," Apolina whispered as she traced her finger down the center of Honey's breasts, now sensitive and swollen with milk since she was seven months pregnant.

Apolina heard Honey's fingers squishing inside of her wetness and wanted to help her. The teen beauty kissed Honey's pink lips and got on top of her very carefully so the baby didn't get hurt. The two hot females' breasts meshed together as Apolina thrust her hand down in between Honey's thick thighs, finding and rubbing her wildly throbbing clitoris. The color went from pale pink to a bursting bright red.

"You ever sixty-nine with a guy?" Honey asked her in

between kisses. Her heart beat faster and she breathed harder.

Apolina nodded. "And I ate his cum. Want me to swallow all of yours?"

"Can we do that? Are you ready for that?" Honey inquired in a pant.

"You make me so turned on with the pregnancy and how beautiful, powerful, and confident you are. So, yeah. I wanna please you. I'll do anything you ask. I really want to eat your pussy," Apolina stated, making Honey hotter.

Apolina got on top of her and kissed her stomach first. Then they got locked into a hot 69. Apolina loved her first taste of pussy. Honey was way more of a seasoned vet. She grabbed both of Apolina's asscheeks, spread them wide and feasted on the cream dripping from her delectable cunt. Honey sucked on that clitoris, slapping it and beating it back and forth with her long tongue. She did it so good…

"Umm, oh god!" Apolina mumbled into Honey's pussy. She kept gasping with the joy of each orgasm Honey gave her. "You're so pretty… and it smells wonderful. Like a mango. You taste salty and sweet too."

"I want to fuck you," Honey demanded. "I just have a *need* to fuck you."

Apolina turned around and Honey stood up. "I have this wonderful strap-on dildo… My husband has a really big dick, and he can cause me a lot of pain while I'm pregnant, even a miscarriage. But this dildo is perfect for my pussy. It has no harness. The small part is short and thick and stays in me while I fuck you with the longer part. You can take eight inches?"

"That's really big but… I think so." She was nervous because 8-inches was big.

The dildo was black and once Honey inserted it inside of herself, she lay on her side while in between Apolina's legs which were wrapped around Honey's waist. Once they were in rhythm, Honey reached down and turned the massager button on to number one."

"Ohhh, that feels so good," Apolina whimpered sexily as Honey B slowly made love to her.

"You taste so fucking lovely!" Honey B couldn't keep her tongue in her mouth. She suckled Apolina all over her ears, her throat, her neck and kept kissing her. "My pussy is dripping!"

"I keep cumming all over your big dick!"

Honey B couldn't get enough of Apolina. They made love for hours. Afterwards they drank tequila and ate fried chicken.

Apolina followed her into the living room and they sat watching "Yellowstone" on Netflix with the "mute" button on.

"So you came all the way from Miami?" Honey asked her.

"Yeah," Apolina nodded. "Y'all had advertisements that was so genuine. I mean no clubs let you keep a hundred percent of everything the girls make. S0, I was like I can dance, trick, private lap dances, whatever, and pocket the money? And I get here, to EDC, and all these rumors swirling."

"About?"

"Us pushin' drugs," Apolina stated. "And how y'all so connected… and untouchable."

"All true," Honey B replied. "The clubs ain't legit. No alcohol license but we set up like we legal."

"We pull up here I'm like O-M-F-G.! 'Is that a friggin' Bugatti!' That's like a fuckin' multi-million-dollar car. And this mansion is the most! A bad ass top notch Spanish bitch pushin' a Lambo… and you chose me out of all them other pretty bitches."

Honey B smiled. "I could tell you was a virgin…"

"I never been with a girl, "Apolina told her. "But I've thought about it, and I'm so

Happy it was like this. Now I'ma hate to go wherever I have to."

"Well…" Honey B started. "Me and my husband share girls. We have a deal. I'm kinda cheating right now but I'll tell him. If you're open to it. He's a man's man. He's tall, dark, he switches from gold to all diamond platinum in his grill. He's ex-military, his body is chiseled. He's fuckin' jacked."

"Mm!" Apolina felt lustful for him already. "A man like that and you don't get

Jealous when he's inside of another girl?"

"When he cheats, I do," Honey said "He has the biggest, sweetest, chocolate dick, mami. And I love seeing it plunge into tight white girls, and girls lighter than him… That does something to me."

"I'd be jealous," Apolina admitted. "He's a great lovemaker?"

"That man's dick be deep in my soul…" Honey B stated with emotion. "That's where this baby came from. I knew the *second* I was pregnant…"

"I need to tell you something," the young girl said. "I'm the great grand daughter of Manuel Noriega."

Honey B used her phone to Google search who Manuel Noriega was. "The Panamanian General, connected to the CIA and Pablo Escobar in the eighties and nineties?"

Apolina nodded. "Just wanted to tell you so there's no secrets …

"Okay…" Honey stated slowly. "Well, General Noriega was a cocaine, President. He's gone now."

Apolina laid her head on Honey B's lap, cupping her stomach. "I'd love to have a home here, help with your baby, and be a sex servant to you and your husband. I'll do anything you want."

Honey B leaned down and softly kissed her. "Just remember one thing. It's me you're loyal to. Don't Forget that. Don't you ever fuckin' forget that."

The warning was clear.

CHAPTER FOURTEEN

The Secret Airbase
Custer, South Dakota
Tuesday Evening

CIA black operative and international arms dealer Lieutenant Sampson Gates met Ghostman at the front entrance of the clandestine paramilitary base in Custer, South Dakota. It was 16 degrees Fahrenheit and the wind chill factor was below zero. Prior to leaving the airplane he'd flown in on Ghostman dressed as if he were about to climb Mt. Everest.

"I'm sorry about your fallen comrades," Gates expressed his condolences. "Monk, N9NE, Chief, Fast Eddie, Mustafa and War. I heard everything."

Ghostman nodded. "Thank you."

"The others are inside the barracks," Gates told him. They began the short walk to the main building where they were met by two walking men dressed in full camouflage tactical gear. They were both blond with the look of seasoned killers in their eyes.

Ghostman looked back over his shoulder. "Who're those men?"

"Rangers," Gates kept it short. "Hand-picked by me."

They walked down a long corridor, out the back door where another Ranger was stationed, and right into the "Barrack Post 1" outbuilding. Loud talking could be heard, Pop Smoke's *"Into The Night"* was wafting through Bose speakers.

"Ghostman Dinero! What's up bay-bay!!" Divine boomed loudly when Ghost and Gates came through the doors.

"What up, niggas?!" Ghostman smiled and started hugging and dappin' up all his comrades.

The barracks were packed: Bonecrusher, Knarf, Boo, Knox, Broliks, Bushwacker, Breach, Goliath, Ceasar, Bible, Blackout, Barricade, Ironhide, Devastator, Starscream, Rebel One, Blackbird, Darkstar, Raptor, La Colombiana, and Joker himself.

"Oh shit – *Red?*" Ghostman was surprised.

The two men hugged.

"Whattaya doin'?" Ghostman asked in a quiet tone.

"What the fuck you mean what I'm doin' nigga?" Joker shot back coldly. "I'm here."

"I see that," Ghostman said, shaking his head. "You need

to be back in Chi-Raq, straightening out that mess with Butterfly and finding out who bombed us."

That Butterfly comment infuriated Joker. He wasted no time in punching Ghostman dead in the mouth! Recovering quickly, Ghost side-stepped a second blow and landed a right to Joker's left ear! Joker, a street brawler, put his hands up in that 1986 Mike Tyson style and rushed Ghostman, throwing nothing but powerful blows to his head and body!

The EIE men and Lt. Sampson Gates formed a circle and started yelling, urging the fighters on!

"That's what I'm talkin' bout," Ghostman taunted Joker. "Let's get it den!"

Joker caught him with an uppercut but Ghostman faked like he was hurt! When

Joker came in closer for the kill, Ghost hit him in the jaw so hard it buckled him! Ghostman pummeled Joker after that and down to the ground he went!

"Nah, mufucka, get up!" Ghostman shouted, grand-standing.

Joker shook it off, his mouth dripping blood. "You hit like a ho, nigga. Let's rock!"

Joker rushed back in, delivering a devastating blow to Ghostman's stomach then another upward blast to his ribs! Seeing his face wince up in pain Joker knew Ghost had a hard time inhaling! So, he hit the big dark-skinned man in the midsection again, causing Ghost to back up – to buy time! "Uhn – Uhn! " Joker told him, moving in on him. "Don't run, now!"

Ghostman threw a wild haymaker with his right leaving

his chin wide open for the uppercut that Joker smashed his lights out with! Ghostman crumpled to the cold barracks floor out cold!

"Go get my niggas, Gates," Joker said taking a deep breath. "We'll meet you in the hangar in five... when sleeping beauty here decides to wake up." He pointed at Ghostman.

Ghostman did wake up seconds later, very upset that Joker attacked him in the first place. Joker left the fight on the floor, where his blood was also.

They all went inside of the hangar several minutes later where the two white C-40 clipper passenger jets sat alongside the two MH-47 Chinook Multi-mission helicopters. Lieutenant Gates came into the hangar with eighteen young black men.

"That's Smoke, Rome, Brook and Little Jimmie 2 Tymes!" Knarf laughed, clearly glad at seeing them. "We know you lil mufuckas from Brooklyn!"

"That's Jokers family," Boo realized.

"That's right," Joker acknowledged. "All eighteen of these niggas are my cousins or nephews on my mom and pops' sides of the family. This is Young Army."

EIE Young Army were the ones scrapping and scraping on the streets which lead to the monumental financial successes of EIE when Joker stopped hitting banks and concentrated on their narcotic-laced paper products and their crystal meth heroin. Young Army moved meth empire and cocaine all throughout the Northeast.

"Aight, so they ya Fam but I don't get it, Playboy,"

Ghostman spoke up, still fuming from the loss he took in the fight with Joker. "Why are they in South Dakota?"

"To train, "Joker quipped.

"For what?" Ghostman probed.

"That's my business," Joker told him. "Speakin' of which every soldier in the organization must train. Military training, camps, the whole nine."

Most of the men scoffed.

"Everyone I know love and care about will be immune from prosecution," Joker told them. "Your decision. You wanna evade taxes, own military grade weapons, have a life of crime and luxury, then this is the ultimatum. They givin' us the license to steal and kill on one end… on the other we play by their rules."

"Okay, let's get it," Knarf said. "I'm done talkin'."

"C'mon," Lt. Gates waved at the men to follow him.

What he showed them made their eyes pop out of their heads.

CHAPTER FIFTEEN

The Secret Airbase
Tuesday 9:00 PM

Lieutenant Sampson Gates led the group of 40 (22 EIE Army, 18 Young Army) into a sectioned-off portion of the hangar where several aviation mechanics were readying one of the Clippers for flight. Gates used the smaller double doors to go outside towards the airstrip.

"Special delivery," Gates presented to them.

Joker and the others were instantly impressed at all the weapons and vehicles being unloaded off of military transport trucks and two 18-wheeler flatbeds. Once everything was on the ground Joker and his men inspected everything.

"The money I paid you covered all this shit?" Joker wondered aloud.

"Somewhat," Gates replied. "This is all standard Ranger weapons and equipment."

He handed Joker an iPad with the equipment inventory on it. It read:

250-M-4 Carbine.

12-84 mm Ranger Antitank Weapons Systems.

10 -60 mm, 81mm and 120 mm mortars.

100 – M240B Machine Guns.

50 – Mark 19 RP MM Grenade Launchers.

10-Javelin Portable missile systems.

4 – Unmanned Aerial Vehicles.

6 – Ground Mobility Vehicle- R's.

. Tactical Internet.

. All-terrain Vehicles.

. Grenadier Brat.

Joker walked over to one of the UAV's and looked over at Gates. His men had the very same expressions on their faces.

"You thinkin' the same thing I'm thinkin'?" Boo whispered to Joker.

"Javelin Missile systems?" Joker said to Gates. "UAV's… This shipment looks like it got lost."

"Are we going to Afghanistan?" Bonecrusher had a serious look on his face. "Javelins? Mortars?"

Lt. Gates shrugged. "Whattaya want from me? I work for them, too. They said to deliver this package and I delivered."

"You delivered mass casualty war weapons," Joker told him.

"There will be more packages delivered," Nina Overstreet said, suddenly appearing wearing a fully padded camouflage snowsuit. "You never know when you'll need the other options. Remember Nyomi Malek?"

"And her partner Brayson?" Joker asked.

"FBI agents don't have partners," Nina corrected him. "Nyomi is from the FBI Counter- Terrorism Division."

"Big game hunters," Bonecrusher said slowly.

"Welcome to the big leagues," Nina announced. "Today it's Xanaphoulous, tomorrow it could be us heading through a Mexican cartel tunnel and into the Sonora Desert seeking out and destroying a terrorist cell. We have been tracking a particular group of terrorists who are planning to enter America through drug cartel tunnels. So, I wouldn't be surprised at the equipment delivery in the future boys."

"Send a SEAL hit unit to stop 'em," Boo said.

Nina sighed. "We've alerted the Hondurans, the Mexicans… they know that Interpol has these particular individuals red-flagged, yet no one has stopped them. These are exactly the kinds of threats we lose sleep over."

They all headed back inside to warm up.

"Get some rest," Nina advised Joker. "Who knows if tomorrow will be a good and easy day…"

"Hm," Joker uttered. "We in the wrong business if we looking for easy." He was still thinking of that shipment and what it had in it. Four UAV'S (drones), mortars, Javelins, etcetera. *With the CIA involved I should have known some big things were coming down the pipe,* he thought.

The Twin Towers
Wednesday Afternoon

CHAPTER SIXTEEN

The Twin Towers
Wednesday Afternoon

Meanwhile, telephone calls were flooding into Chicago from New York nonstop…

Don Braga was being informed that his niece, Detective Hanna Genovese, was robbed and killed in Brooklyn. Several family members and "made members" called him to offer their sincerest condolences. A murdered NYPD detective was a huge deal anywhere in America, especially in the Big Apple.

Other telephone calls were coming from Joker's cousin O'Mira. She was trying desperately to contact him and tell him that her mother was missing but his cellphone kept going directly to voicemail. That's because, like every other EIE/Young Army member no digital devices were permitted on missions.

Uzenna returned home to the Twin Towers from the doctor's office where she tested negative for Covid-19. On her way back she'd made reservations on American Airlines Flight 303 from Chicago's O'Hare Airport to Jacksonville, Mississippi.

She wanted to pack up all of her belongings, but she had tons of clothes, handbags, etc. So, to look less suspicious she, instead, took only a single key to a safe deposit box and her best Birkin bag.

"C'mon, Junior." she smiled as she reached for her and Joker's son. She already had a baby bag packed up for him.

"You're going out with him?" The Mexican nanny asked her.

"Yeah, we'll be right back," she lied. Uzenna knew that Joker and the nanny were especially tight, so she didn't trust telling her anything.

Amelia hesitated. "I get ready to come."

"You stay," Uzenna ordered her.

"Mr. Joker ordered I not let him out of my sight," Amelia was firm. "I come."

Uzenna smiled uncomfortably for a quick second then relented. "Okay."

Uzenna left the young woman and, seconds later she returned.

WWWHHHAAAPPP!!

BONNNGGG!!

While Amelia had her back turned Uzenna produced a hammer and brought it down had with one hand on top of her head! And, to make it count, she hit the stunned nanny again, this time behind the right ear. Amelia fell to the floor unconscious and bleeding from the two wounds in her head. Fortunately for Amelia she wasn't hit that hard.

Uzenna bundled up her baby and beelined it straight out of the building to a waiting Uber vehicle before Amelia could come to.

"First, to BMO Harris Bank," she instructed the female driver. "I'll need you to wait for a hundred-dollar tip. And then to O'Hare."

She was taken to the bank first where she removed a manila envelope stuffed with stacks of paper-banded cash from one of the safe deposit boxes. First, she stared in disbelief at the money and then went back into the safe deposit box, disappointed at the amount. She'd thought there would be more inside of the box.

"Shit."

She exited the bank and returned to her Uber ride. Taking a deep breath, she ordered the driver to take her to the airport. *It'll have to be enough for now,* she thought quietly. She barely had $30,000 in cash but she did have money secretly stashed in an account in Belize. She just had to make sure it *appeared as if* she were returning to Mississippi. Once Joker realized she was gone with his son he'd hunt her down and have her killed.

The honey-skinned beauty wished she had been able to

keep her mouth shut when she had spoken so recklessly towards her husband, calling him a coward in front

of others. Words she knew she could not come back from. *You knew that man was a ruthless, cold-blooded killer and now he'll be coming after you with all of his power.*

It was either run while she still had the chance to or stay stuck, like a sitting duck, waiting for a bullet to the head. At least with running she felt like she and her son had a chance.

L. A. County Fairgrounds
Pomona, California
Thursday 3:50 AM

CHAPTER SEVENTEEN

L. A. County Fairgrounds
Pomona, California
Thursday 3:50 AM

The Clipper landed at a CIA Black site in Pomona, California, Thursday morning at 3:50 AM. From there they boarded a school bus that transported them to the Los Angeles County Fairgrounds.

"What's this?" Casci Caliendo asked the other EIE members as the bus rolled to a stop.

Nyomi Malek spoke up. "These are the UC vehicles on lease so, please, do not damage them, smoke in them…"

Everyone ignored her and got off of the bus carrying their own bags, carry-on cases, etcetera.

"For a while I was expectin' all-terrain vehicles, Humvees, maybe even a Stryker." Bonecrusher commented, a hint of sarcasm dripping from his tone.

There were an entire line of what could only be described as luxury cars, vans and SUV's parked side by side.

First, there was a charcoal black Himalaya Specter (Defender). It was all muscle, 500HP, automatic, beautiful. Next to it was a black Mountain JLU Rubicon Edition Wrangler; a Ram AEV Prospector XL, three Mercedes Benz G550's (black, white and blue) a Hummer HI Alpha and two awesome Mercedes-Benz Sprinter 3500 EXT'S.

Brayson Bailey showed up as everyone was loading up and preparing to roll out.

"What's up?" Nyomi jumped out of the Sprinter to speak to him. "I thought you were sitting on the sub's (subject's) hideout."

They walked away from the group.

"Bone," Knarf stared at his comrade. "Did you really think we'd be using Humvees with military grade equipment on em – out here?"

"And a *Stryker* battalion," Joker added.

Bone shrugged, hopping into the driver's seat of the blue G-wagon. "I'm dyin' for a real ground war. Where we destroy the city and massacre everyone. This shit ain't even a warm-up for us."

"Ghengis Khan-ass nigga," Joker commented.

"Hey, Red?" Nyomi called out to him. "Wanna come over here for a minute?"

"Yeah," he said and walked over to where the two FBI

agents were standing near the Lincoln Navigator, he'd pulled up in.

Bone, Knarf, Boo, Knox, Broliks, Bush, Breach, Goliath, Ceasar, Bible, Blackout, Barricade, Ironhide, Devastator, Starscream, Rebel, Blackbird, Darkstar, Raptor, Ghostman, and Casci all observed the trio as they huddled up, wondering what they were talking about. A few minutes later they found out.

"O'Mira's panickin' that Minnie has gone missing," Joker revealed. "Leah shot a text to me through Brayson. There's also news of the robbery-murder of Detective Genovese.

Casci gasped. "Don Braga's niece?"

Joker nodded. "Leah also said Uzenna's in the wind with my mufuckin' son."

"We'll be fine with you leaving to handle your personal affairs," Nyomi told him.

"I'm good," Joker said, his face stoic.

"As long as your head's in the game because this guy we're after is bad," Nyomi reminded them. "Real bad."

Joker nodded. "My head's in the fuckin game, woman. As for bad… Nobody badder than us. Let's go." He drew cheers from his squad.

"He's set up behind a powerful wall of criminals here in a section of Pomona called Ghostown," Brayson said "There's an entire block of businesses they own on West Donahue Boulevard. One of them is a hair and nail salon with a large upstairs space the organization uses for pornographic production involving minors."

"American girls?" Joker asked.

"Many of them are Ukrainian, Albanian and others have been identified as 'American missing,' runaways, things like that," Brayson explained as a black Equinox quietly rolled up and parked next to Brayson's vehicle.

"It's Nina," Casci, said.

"Hm." Joker wasn't stupid. Something more was at play here. "Any of the American girls black or Latina?"

Brayson appeared stuck. "Well, there's forty-plus girls we suspect are American. Some as young as fourteen."

"How many are white Nyomi?" Joker pressed her.

His entire group listened intently, wondering what was up.

Nyomi didn't hesitate. "I believe all of them," she admitted.

Joker smiled. "Why the fuck are we here? With the fuckin CIA on-scene? Hm? This should be a routine Title 18, Section 1591, FBI raid, or a Megan's Law operation. What I don't understand is why we have orders to neutralize this Xanaphoulous."

Nina had been standing quietly next to her car, but she'd heard enough. "Nobody ordered you to understand anything except your orders! Now if you're done let's finish up here and complete the objective."

Joker looked directly into her unflinching eyes.

"He's one of yours, huh?" Joker surmised. "What – he know too much? Did he whistle blow like Snowden or Assange – on your Director? What're y'all tryna hide from the American people?"

"You're acting like a kid," Nina accused him.

"You're acting *like* we're kids," Joker accused her in return. "When this is Amerikkikan soil, y'all have evidence of these peoples crimes … the FBI could call up their HRT elite squad and have everyone in handcuffs, with your lilly little white missing girls free. At least have the *respect* to tell us and *why* we're being sent in to kill and not capture."

Nina walked away, inviting Joker to follow her.

"Look," Nina whispered to him. "Xanaphoulous was or is a CIA operative who has close ties to Russian oligarchs and powerful military leaders with knowledge of Russian nuclear activities. But he went off the grid and the Director lost trust in his ability to funnel useful information back to the U.S. in fact, it is believed that Xanaphoulous has been feeding the Russians NATO secrets."

"NATO secrets," Joker repeated. "How would-?"

She hesitated. "The CIA has a Program where we recruit girls straight out of high school and train them to speak fluent Russian, they live in Kiev, Moscow, those cities. We turn them into very highly paid escorts for the rich and powerful. They look like baby faced school girls on their websites, but they are spies and killers. Xanaphoulous knows about this program."

"How?"

"He developed it." Nina looked at him.

Joker understood. "Not stoppin' this nigga will place the program in jeopardy."

"Not to mention every escort in it," she added.

"No Guantanamo Bay for this guy," Joker stated.

"For none of them," Nina said clearly. "As unusual as it is

seeing the EIE General on the ground … it's good that you're here."

"Yeah?" Joker lit up a cigar as they spoke. "Why's that?"

"So there's no misunderstanding, "Nina said, a coldness in her eyes. "You'll have fifteen minutes to sweep, kill and burn down every structure on the block. Don't harm the women. You won't have FBI or law enforcement assistance or interference."

"What about 9- 1-1 calls?"

"We're jamming all cellphone calls, landline and internet in the area," she told him. Joker was wildly surprised "You'll do all that?"

"We're the Federal government," she reminded him. "We can do whatever we want."

"Okay, c'mon!" Joker turned back to his team of mercenaries. "This mission is bigger and riskier than we first thought. Let's see that map…"

Though no one knew it at the time, the upcoming confrontation with the rogue CIA operative, Marcellus Xanaphoulous, would come at a deadly cost.

CHAPTER EIGHTEEN

Ghostown Pomona

Thursday 5:00 PM

"*Black luxury van coming your way, over,*" Darkstar reported over the headset- earpiece he wore. He sat scoping out the semi-quiet Taylor Boulevard and National Avenue in the "Ghostown" section of Pomona, California.

They had set up a one square mile recon radius around the block of businesses Marcellus Xanaphoulous – or "Maxi" for short - - and his Serbian henchmen had set up all along, west Donahue Boulevard.

"*We got eyes, copy that,*" Joker Red acknowledged. Further up Taylor Boulevard Joker was already out on foot with the tall, leggy, blond bombshell Casci "La Colombiana" Caliendo. They we're already out on foot walking, across Taylor and heading diagonally through the deserted parking lot of an old Circle K store. *"We're on West Donahue, over,"* Joker's voice came through over the entire squad's headset and earpieces.

"Crazy fucker," Ghostman said, shaking his head. He was inside of the Himalaya Specter with Bonecrusher, Knarf and Bible Reed. "He shouldn't even be here."

"He thinks he should," Knarf replied, itching to jump out and buss off the M-4 Carbine he was gripping between his legs. "What do you think, Bible?"

At first it looked like the big, dark, gargantuan man would stay silent. "Proverbs 13: 3 says *'In the mouth of the foolish is a red of pride; but the lips of the wise shall preserve them,'"* Bible quoted slowly.

"You mean the shit Uzenna said," Knarf mentioned. "Callin' him a coward and all?"

Bible sighed. "Bible just say what's in Holy Bible. *'But he knoweth not that the dead are there; and that her guests are in the depths of hell'* Proverbs 9:18."

"That black luxury van contained six nicely dressed females and two men in dark business suits, over," Joker reported again. *"Approaching a bar to my right, not many inside, but most likely Serbian hittaz. Across the street to my left there is a small mini-market with a self-serve car wash next to it. We're bein' watched, over."*

"No shit," Nina Oversteet muttered from the confines of her black Equinox. Nyomi and Brayson were with her and had heard him, too.

"Walkin' past the nail salon," Joker transmitted. *"Can't fuckin see shit, over."*

"How close did *you* guys get? "Nina, the Black CIA agent, asked Agent Branson Bailey.

"Not that close, "the FBI agent said with an incredulous expression on his face. "Get him outta there!" He sounded alarmed.

"What?!" Nina scoffed at the suggestion. "Let it play out."

Brayson didn't like it. "Those savages have snipers on the rooftops," He cautioned.

Nina ignored him.

"I have eyes on Maxi," Joker transmitted minutes later. *"He's upstairs in the studio above the salon. As we walked away, I heard a girl screaming and glass break. We need to move now, over! Move!"*

"That's a negative, Red, negative!" Nina issued the override. *"Back to the rendezvous and I'll tell you why, over!"* She commanded.

"What the fuck!" Joker was livid.

He and Casci strolled on through the block and, as planned, were picked up by the team in the black Rubicon Wrangler driven by Devastator. All other team members were rounded up and, once again, they gathered at the Los Angeles County Fairgrounds.

Joker glared at the dark chocolate skinned CIA agent. "Why'd you abort, Overstreet?" he demanded. "We were ready to rock! Why'd you stop us?!"

"I didn't," she reported, looking up into the skies above and pointing. "They did."

"A drone?" Joker looked up but didn't see anything. "I don't see it. A spy plane. I don't see nothing."

"And you won't," she stated. *"We* won't."

Joker wasn't surprised. "What y'all get up there? A U2 Dragon Lady? An E-9A Widget, AWACS, what?"

"Neither." She shook her head. "EC- 130J Commando Solo III."

"Goddamn," Ghostman muttered at hearing that. "Electronic Warfare Aircraft. "He looked at Joker.

"That's how y'all jammin' cellphone towers and phone calls temporarily," Joker said. "Why'd *they* abort?"

She was checking her laptop as he spoke and replied. *"Technical issues over,* they report. Let's go!"

They all climbed into their vehicles and headed in the direction of the target.

"Red, "Ghostman said in a low voice. "That Commando Solo Three is one of the best Electronic Warfare Aircraft on the planet."

Joker nodded. It demonstrates how serious this DOD/CIA deal really is.

CHAPTER NINETEEN

Uzenna & Junior
Belize City, Belize
Thursday 4 PM

U zenna settled her and Junior into the small shore Hotel nicely. She inspected the room. It had a nice queen-sized bed; a clean fresh look and the bathroom was good quality. At $125 per night, which she paid in cash, she had to be careful. She only had $30,000-hardly enough to splurge on as though she had no common sense. She had to play it smart.

"C'mon stinky boy," she said to her baby after she removed his shitty diaper. He found amusement in everything it seemed. "So, it's funny?" She asked him.

They showered together. Uzenna was sad, frustrated, and emotionally drained. This life on the run was not one she'd had a lot of time to plan out. But she had street grit, and instincts, so there was no doubt she'd survive.

After they were dressed in pajamas they ate and then crashed out for the entire night. When she woke up, she used a burner to call Iani, her older sister.

"Girl, where the fuck you at?" Iani asked, glad to hear from her "Y'all okay?"

"Where is *he*?" Uzenna shot back quickly.

"On a mission with them government people," Iani revealed, worry in her voice. "Why the hell you couldn't shut up?!" She lamented.

"I don't know," Uzenna sighed, looking at her son gnawing on a pretzel stick as he lay on the bed. "Hurt over Romie … I'm not sure."

That comment seemed to anger Iani. "Well, now look! You on the run… with his *infant* son! His first-born, and you think he won't find you?! He's a DOD- CIA contractor now! Words matter. He was what we wanted him to be. You, me, the other girls. But you had to turn his ironclad ego into wet toilet paper with all that shit you said and now he's on the frontlines!"

"Look," Uzenna told her, exasperation in her tone. "It is what it is right?! I feel like I can't walk it back whether I want to or not.

"Do you want to?"

"Umm," Uzenna hesitated. "He's gonna kill me. That's

what I feel and … I'm not so sure about everything anymore."

"Meanin'? "

"Let's keep it real," Uzenna started. "This family is not about family, or love. It's about sex. And he ain't even happy wit that. He crazier about that doctor bitch than anything."

Iani had heard enough. "Whattaya want from me cuz you sound like a jealous high school chick right now."

"Whateva," Uzenna scoffed. "You be a fool, stay a fool.

"We were Mafia *whores*," Iani pointed out. "Since *kids*. We have a *sex circle* of all girls. You meet the right gangster the right time, and he's your hero. He's all our hero … and he's *beautiful*. A machine in bed and we hand him all of us as the prize. Three bad black girls, a bad Chinese girl, and nine bad snow bunnies. And we all *agree* to get pregnant, to build somethin' we never had. Stability. A Family."

"But he gets to Fuck all of us – and Tithi- but once Romie does it to one dude!!!" she trailed off, starting to cry. "Man, I'm through…"

"I'm hurt over all that shit, too," Iani professed. She held back her tears. "But betrayal like that from not just her but an EIE comrade? He saw it as catchin' his brother Al fuckin you. And, when we chose to execute for that betrayal, we did so outta the *survival* of the twelve left… and these thirteen babies. Not to mention the money, the cars, houses… the life, the-"

"*The sex*," Uzenna reminded her emphatically.

"Bitch so what?" Iani replied. "I get to nut more than ever

with all these pretty bitches comin' around. As Jokers wives we get our pick off the top. But me and you…"

Uzenna waited. *"Me and you…?"*

"I can never replace that forbidden fruit taste in my mouth," Iani admitted. "No pussy smells as good as my little sister's."

"Mm." Iani definitely had Uzenna thinking.

"You need to come home and fix this mess you made," Iani warned her. "Don't make him have to find you. And his son."

"Alright look", Uzenna said, wanting to wrap it up. "I'll call you back in a couple of days. I may of may not need money. I haveta check something out first."

They hung up. Her next call was to her investment banker in Belize City where she'd been stashing money at. Her hope was to withdraw all of it on short notice before she could disappear where Joker could not find her.

Ghostown

5:46 PM

CHAPTER TWENTY

Ghostown

5:46 PM

Ghostman, La Colombiana, Bonecrusher, Joker Red and Caeser were the first group to set it off. As they burst through the front doors of the Ma Cherie Nail Salon on west Donahue Boulevard, rapid machine gun fire was already erupting up the street behind them.

Boo, explosive specialist Frank "Knarf "Brown, Knox and Broliks were shooting it out with Serbian gunmen at the bar. That particular shootout was disastrous from the start because a Serbian sniper on a rooftop across the street got of a volley of great shots. One of them hit Knarf in the back of his head!

Four Serbian henchman were able to take cover inside of the bar while returning fire! Boo, seeing that Knarf was down, knew that his group was in trouble.

"Fall back!" He yelled to Hard Knox and Broliks. "Fall back!"

They cleared the entrance and Boo popped several grenades before throwing them into the bar. He crouched down to take cover alongside the cement wall below the window. KABOOOM!! KABAOOM!! KABOOOM!!

The triple blasts were deafening.

Broliks and Knox threw stun grenades inside before they entered as a precaution. Moments later, donning MP5's, they burst in and swept the premises for more fighters.

"Uhhh," a man groaned from beneath a table. He lay in a pool of blood. The shrapnel had pierced his face, chest and side but he was still alive.

Boo one-handed the MP5 and shot the writhing Serb dead with a three-round burst to the belly! In the rear of the bar, near the office area," he yelled out, "I got somethin' back here!"

Broliks and Knox hurried back to where Boo was. What they saw didn't surprise them. There were two white females, probably teenagers, handcuffed and naked. Their feet were tied to a steel radiator. Both girls, brunettes, very pretty, seemed to be too calm after hearing the grenades going off up front. Not to mention all the machine gun fire – they were almost catatonic.

"They're doped up!" Boo said, looking into both girls' eyes with a pin light. "We gotta go out back with them or risk getting hit by that sniper! Let's move, get them to safety and return for the rest of this fight!"

<hr>

THE NAIL SALON

"All hands on deck at the salon!" Joker was barking out the order over the radio. *"All hands on deck at the salon! And somebody needs to take out those snipers!"*

Blackbird, Darkstar, Rebel and Starscream – who'd been covering the front and rear of the nail salon/porn production site-turned their attention to the rooftops across the street, facing the salon. Starscream spotted a small reflection of light bounce off of what he figured was the high-powered telescope of one of the snipers.

Starscream ran like a demon across the street and searched out an entrance to the large multi-floor industrial building. Blackbird, Darkstar and Rebel soon followed. They were hot on the tail of both snipers.

"Marcellus Xanaphoulous!" Ghostman yelled up the stairs that led to the illicit movie production studio. "This is the FBI! We have you surrounded! Give it up so no one else gets hurt!"

Upstairs, Marcellus opened up the door and shoved a female out of it! She rolled and tumbled down the stairs! Joker and Colombiana both reached for her and pulled her out of harm's way but what they saw was horrifying, even to them!

"Fuck!" Colombiana gasped.

The girl could be no older than 16. Blond, slender, milky white skin with dark, bruised, track marks visible on both arms. She was dead from a single, small caliber, gunshot wound to the temple. She'd been murdered by Xanaphoulous.

Inside of the studio were twelve more frightened young women. Marcellus had been there watching on orgy involving his own half dozen henchmen while a 4-man camera crew had caught it all an video and live stream.

"That's not FBI!" Marcellus growled to his men. He went to the door. "I have twelve more these Ukrainian whores and U.S. whores up here! You are not FBI! You leave now or I kill all!"

The bushy eyebrowed Serb was 100% crazy. He lobbed a grenade down the stairs and as soon as they heard it hit midway down, they automatically knew.

"*Grenade!*" Someone yelled.

They ran and fell flat to the floor.

KABOOOM!!

"*Alpha Team respond, over,*" Starscream radioed Joker, Ghostman, Colombiana, Bonecrusher and Ceasar.

"*Alpha responding, over,*" Colombiana said back as she looked around to make sure her comrades were okay.

"*Sniper one and two have been neutralized, over,*" Starscream reported.

"Aww, nooo," she whispered as she crawled to where

Ghostman and the others were crouched around Bonecrusher's body.

Boo, Hard Knox, Broliks, Blackbird, Darkstar, Rebel and Starscream all appeared. The dark skinned, pop-eyed, man name Boo was out of breath as he checked Bonecrusher's pulse.

"What happened?" Boo asked.

"Looks like shrapnel tore straight through his heart," Ghostman stated icily. "Son, we have been here too long. They can only use cellphone and web jammin' technology for so long."

Joker radioed Nina. *"Alpha here. Can we get that time extended by ten minutes? Over."*

No answer.

"Black Panther you there, over," Joker called again.

"Black Panther copy," Nina came back. *"That request is negative, Alpha. You hove six minutes, over."*

"Omega, over." Joker radioed Bushwacker, Breach, Goliath, and Bible. *"Omega, come in."*

Bushwacker responded. *"Omega here, over."*

"Bring in the Javelins, over." Joker ordered.

"Hey, boss," Boo said. "We lost Knarf."

Everyone heard that and got quiet.

A minute later Bushwacker and his team was on scene with the Javelin rocket launchers.

"One in the back," Joker pointed. "Go! The other in the front upstairs, second floor!"

Thirty seconds later they were both in position.

"One, two, three, fire!!" Joker ordered, but he felt nauseated

doing it because those rockets would kill nearly everybody up there. He wanted to save those girls but there was no time, and the mission objective was to kill Marcellus and all of his men.

The twin explosions were like the boom of angry thunder. B-B-BABOOOM!! B-B-BABOOOM!! At first it seemed like the ceiling above would fall down on top of them! The door up the stairs had been blown off the hinges and the smell of acidic smoke and debris was heavily clouding the air!

"Ironhide, Devastator, Barricade, Blackout move in with the vehicles!" Joker barked the orders. *"Knarf is down! Bone is down! Collect them first, over!"*

Five of the women had survived but they had injuries. The other women were dead, killed by the rockets. Marcellus was not there!

"Maxi is on the loose! I repeat Maxi is on the loose, over," Joker was outraged. *"He's gotta be on the roof! Look!"*

And, sure enough, there was an open door that led up to the roof.

"I got this mufucka." Joker said, reloading his MP5. "Y'all pack it up and go!""

He bolted out after the rogue CIA black op.

As soon as he hit the rooftop Joker noticed the blood trail. Marcellus was wounded. Joker smiled. The building was connected to other structures but that didn't matter. Marcellus was losing a lot of blood. Not drops but splotches.

Each time he had to cross over onto a different roof he had to climb or jump up onto a higher wall. The wall leading to the top of the bar business was no different. Once Joker ran and sailed clearly over it he had eyes on Marcellus.

"FBI. Ha!" He laughed sarcastically and threw up blood. He was sitting down with a strange-looking Beretta in his right hand. "If you FBI... I'm rapper Eminem. "

"Tell me somethin'," Joker said to him coming continuously closer. "Why these young women? *Kids* for fucksakes?"

"You don't know anything about your government," Marcellus said, having a hard time breathing. He had a bad stomach wound. "I only follow orders given by CIA! They sent soldiers to kill me, hm? Today: me. Tomorrow: you."

And with that, he raised the Beretta to his head and blew his own noodles out!

"Ayo, you good?" Ghostman shouted from the next roof over.

"Yeah!" Joker said and picked up the Serbian made Beretta. "Yeah, he dead."

"Alright, then, let's ride!" Ghostman said.

Gas drum firebombs were placed inside each business and, as they made their escape, the bombs were set off. West Donahue became a raging inferno within minutes. The FBI swept in to seize the crime scene and make any evidence of the DOD/CIA's "extrajudicial execution" squad disappear.

Later that night, on their flight back to the South Dakota air base Joker thought about Maxi's final words...

Today: me. Tomorrow: you.

CHAPTER TWENTY-ONE

A Week Later
Brooklyn NY
Saturday Evening

Joker not only threw a double funeral – fit for kings – for Bonecrusher and Knarf, but he did so in Brooklyn where he knew their hearts, their children and their families dwelled.

Bonecrusher was actually born Dwayne Walker and most of his family was from Noble Drew Ali Plaza Projects in Brownsville. But as a child, he was constantly at Fort Greene Projects visiting cousins which is how he first linked up with Ghostman and Knarf. And through them all the other members of "Everything Is Everything" clique.

Knarf was actually Frank spelled backwards. Frank Brown had been called Knarf because of his big pug-like nose and funny looking face. He was a Fort Greene Project native and came from a very large family. He had been a soldier, gangster, and mercenary to the core and like many EIE members, he took extraordinary care of his loved ones, women and children. Still, Joker Red had suitcases full of cash given out to all of his peoples and to Bonecrusher's as well.

The dinner party was held at a fabulous Airbnb brownstone mansion in nearby downtown Brooklyn. The house was owned by a canned fruit and vegetable millionaire who had as many homes as some people had pairs of shoes. In lieu of having one particular caterer provide food for the party guests, Joker Red had asked Tithi to handle it. And she showed off…

She took the opportunity to have several different restaurants deliver. First, *Lodi* came through with some high-end neighborhood Italian food from Rockefeller Center. *Ci Siamo*, known for their tasty Italian comfort foods arrived with literally hundreds of dishes: stracci with rabbit ragù and a caramelized onion torta was most talked about. *Temple Bar*, from out of SoHo, brought a "little" food and lended Tithi a bartender for the night.

She even had Les Trois Chevaux from West Village show up with some French food like their tasty truffle soup. But her personal favorite was the Indian food at Dhamaka. Tithi was cool with chef Chintan Pandya who was well known for his award-winning spice lamb ribs.

Tithi had Dhamaka delivered more than 150 slabs of delicious lamb ribs.

"I like what you did, baby," Joker complemented Tithi as they fed each other on the master bedroom balcony. "They seem to be eatin' more and drinkin' less."

"You said limit the alcohol, so I did," Tithi grinned. "And it works."

"This food must be really expensive," he said.

She shrugged, knowing he wasn't really worried about it. "I'm sorry about Crusher and Knarf."

Tithi had called Bonecrusher "Crusher" because with her Indian accent, saying "Bone" just seemed to come out the wrong way all the time.

"We celebratin' their life, babe," Joker reminded her. "Don't be sorry tonight."

Joker sent a text message out. Moments later his seventeen-year-old nephew, Smoke, from Young Army, walked into the room followed by his brothers Roman and Brook. All three boys were Joker Red's sister' Natasha's kids.

Smoke was the oldest at 17. He was light skinned, tall, well-built and had a lot of respect on the streets. He was good with his hands, and he never hesitated to bust his guns.

Rome was 16, brown skin, he had really good wavy hair and a medium build. He stood at an average height, but he was always the one to fuck the party up by using a gun to either rob somebody, shoot them, or both.

The quiet one was Brook. And though he seemed shy he was anything but. He was only 15 but stood a solid six feet tall and was 175 pounds. He was one of those young bulls who walked around playing "The Knockout Game" on unsuspecting grown men while his brothers and other Young Army members caught it on the cell phone video.

"Natasha here?" Joker asked the boys about his older sister.

"Downstairs dancin', I think," Smoke guessed. "What's happening with it, son?"

They all went out on the balcony.

"Mommie?" Joker nudged her with an elbow.

"Hm?" Tithi looked at him.

"These is my sister Natasha's sons," Joker introduced them. "Smoke, Rome and Brook. This here is my main baby, Tithi Patel."

"No diss, unc, but she bad!" Smoke said.

"Miss Universe," Rome added.

"No cap," Brook had to put in his two cents.

"I know," Joker nodded. "Hey y'all see what it is, right?"

The boys nodded.

"Y'all gon' end up killed out here on these streets," Joker told them. "So, all y'all gon' train for several months and when you come back to New York you will be ready to claim every Borough, Tri State hood, all the college parties, have cops in your pocket, everything. Y'all come back and add numbers to Young Army. I'm gonna put y'all in more power than you ever dreamed of and all these lil amateurs out here – run 'em outta town."

"Click clack," Rome simulated the sound of a gun cocking. "We doin' it."

Joker nodded. "Y'all seen what it was like out there. So

pack up what you think you'll need and be ready to leave in 12 hours. Spread the word."

The boys left.

Tithi was still eating the spicy lamb ribs. Joker watched her as he sent a text out to Nina Overstreet. Now that he was done with the last mission he wrote to Nina: *When's the next one?*

"You'll know when I do," she responded. *"It is time to decompress… like me. I'm at the Boca Raton's adults only Yacht Club. Harborside pool club, many restaurants and bars, a private golden beach and, oh, where I am right now. The spa Palmera."*

"I need a favor."

"?" She wrote back.

"Uzenna Jade Hodges and my infant son named after me. I need them found," he explained. *"We had a bad fallout and now she's afraid of what I'll do."*

"…" She wrote back. *"Send me every detail. But if you hurt this girl so help me god, JR."*

"Promise." But the truth was, Uzenna deserved a bullet in her head…

"Tithi," Joker said, stopping her from eating.

"Hm?" She smiled.

"Look at you!" he laughed. "Lips all greasy. You eatin' at that poor little lamb like a she-wolf!"

"No, I'm not!" She cried, throwing a balled-up napkin at him. "I'm just hungry and these ribs are sooo goood!" She gushed.

"And you are sooo pregnant!" He pointed out.

"How you figure that?" She asked. "I am not pregnant!"

"Come on, man," he smirked. "Thirteen babies? I can't miss. And look at that juicy ass and thighs you got! Mm!"

She walked into his arms. "I love you." They kissed and held each other for what felt like eternity.

CHAPTER TWENTY-TWO

Sunday Morning

At 6:00 AM many of the 300-plus guests had already left but Joker and Tithi was still there. They had fallen asleep after locking and bolting the door. He sat up and looked at Tithi sprawled out next to him wearing nothing but a beige Givenchy tank top and boy shorts that accentuated her lovely cinnamon buttocks. The way she slept with her right knee kicked up, her backside to him, displayed her little pussy print from the rear. He felt himself becoming aroused at the sight of that sexy slice of hers.

He headed into the bathroom and jumped straight into the shower. Once he was done, he dried off, brushed his teeth and everything else. Once dressed, in an expensive designer sweatsuit, and Jordans, he threw on the Rolex Submariner, his double Beretta shoulder holsters and an all-blue New York Yankee jacket.

"Wake up, bae," Joker said swatting Tithi's exposed rump. "Ima go see who's still here and we'll be back."

"Where we goin'? "Tithi asked sitting up.

"Shiid, where don't I have to be?" He said, knowing there was a lot he had to do." I have some things to tie up here with my family. O'Mira's trippin' about her mom bein' missing. I ain't seen Natasha, my other sisters, cousins … and these kids of theirs are fuckin teenagers already."

"You mean your nephews?" Tithi yawned as she walked into the bathroom. He watched how her asscheeks jiggled and knew she has pregnant because Tithi was a petite little thing with a nice little firm bubble butt. Now that ass had some jiggle to it.

"Yeah," he said, watching her closely as she stripped naked. "Oh, shit, new ink?" he asked pointing downwards.

She looked down at her bare right foot and ankle as she peed. "A mother with her two Bengal Tiger cubs. You like it?" she asked.

He nodded. "Hell yeah. What are the flowers and plants?"

She laughed. "You notice everything… Well, have you ever heard of aconite?"

Joker had a superior IQ. "It's a poison from…"

"… The Indian Aconite plant root," she finished for him. "The flower is cute but the root holds an extremely toxic poison."

"Looks amazin'," he complimented her. "Who did it?"

"Um, some Albanian artist Honey B recommended," she stated innocently, hoping he was satisfied with that.

She got into the shower and he left her to it.

"Joker?" Natasha entered the kitchen right after he did.

Natasha Catherine Hodges was brown-skinned, like their father, but she had green eyes like Joker and their mother. Natasha was a thick woman, 5 feet 8 inches tall, 190 pounds, but she had all "killer curves". There was nothing sloppy about her. She had a good job with Verizon as "Advertising Coordinator" and had recently bought a house in Jamaica, Queens.

"These doggone boys all about to either go to jail or die out in the gutter," Natasha told him in a low voice as they sat down to share a bowl of mixed, freshly sliced, fruit and bottles of water.

"I know, Tash," he said, chomping on a mouth full of blueberries and kiwi fruit. "I've taken an interest."

"Mr. Big," she teased him. "You don't show up for parties, barbecues, weddings, graduations – nothin'."

Joker shook his head. "You mean like when one of y'all niggas came to visit me when I was in prison?"

"I sent money," she quipped. "What?" She stared, defiant.

"Except you," he said. "You get a pass."

She nodded. "Now you – Mr. Big… that's what all the fam says anyway."

"Fuck the fam," Joker brushed her off.

"They're scared you."

Joker looked at her. "Well, and then there's that."

"Skeeter," she reminded him. "Remember him?"

"They need to move past it," Joker told her. "You do too."

"I have," she retorted with an attitude. "Whattaya gonna do wit my sons, J.R. Make drug dealers… bank robbers out of –?"

"Make soldiers out of them," he said simply. "They'll be trained and groomed to be soldiers for hire."

Natasha sat back. "You mean like you."

"Like me," he repeated with a sarcastic scoff. "First off I don't have to extend my hand out at all to you or nobody in our mufuckin' family. I'm the hundred-million-dollar winner among us and it don't come from no rigged up Powerball. It comes from my ruthless mind, heart and iron fuckin' nuts. Fuck you mean *like you.*"

"I ain't mean it like that," she said trying to walk it back. "I gotcha back motherfucker. Don't hold it over me for not comin' to see you in prison. Nobody wants to see you in no cage. Fuck you wit that. I was bein' funny cuz of all the girls and the kids and shit like you some cult leader."

"Natasha, you know I scored 200 on the I.Q. Test," he reminded her. "When people say shit- *like you-* in those two words I pick it up. So explain how you want. The toothpaste is out the tube. The bell is rung. Ain't no unringin' it. Aside from you I only go but so far in fuckin' wit our family. Whatever views you have of me—whatever your opinions are—came from moms, pops, our aunts, uncles, cousins, whoever. You formed your thoughts. I'd rather not deal with *nobody* I'm related to but family still means something sacred to me. You was always my little ace growing up and you mean a lot to me. I remember those twenty-, fifty-, and hundred-dollar money orders you sent me when I was locked up."

"Did y'all do that robbery in 2016?" she inquired quietly.

He nodded. "And?"

She shrugged. "Uncle Doc was sayin' how you had Rolexes, Gucci bags, Tiffany jewelry being sold all through the Fort and how y'all had everyone fooled into thinkin' you worked for a high-end moving company."

"Ain't nobody business ya dig?" he stated as he scrolled through his phone to check out the scores for the NBA. "Remember back 2015 when all those baby monkeys came up missing at the Bronx Zoo on Fordham Road."

"Yeah, who don't?" she asked.

"That was us," he admitted with a chuckle. "Twenty baby Chimpanzees."

"Oh my god man-who does that?" she inquired with a wild laugh. "Why? Whatever happened to them?"

Joker had a grin on his face. "They wanted those Chimps back so bad that they put a one-thousand-dollar reward on them if they were returned safely. I returned them through a lawyer. The zoo came with twenty grand cash. We'd let the monkeys run free in a house we leased. It was one of our more elaborate heists, but it was so easy because we knew the Chimps had been borrowed from the San Diego Zoo and Bronx Zoo officials would turn desperate. It was a five-man job."

"Y'all are so crazy," she said while shaking her head.

"I've always dreamed of strength and power to do what the fuck I feel like," he revealed. "Jay-Z, Russell Simmons,

Damon John from *Shark Tank*-the *Karl Kani, FUBU* owner. I wanted their kinda cash in a way where I can own the cops and be untouchable. I made a lot of connections in the Army-and I mean I not only led to a couple hundred men and women, but I met so, so many people. The only thing that got in the way of my time over there was the realization that the United States was busy killin' all *brown* mufuckas. Each mission we go on I was pocketin' gold, platinum, diamond jewelry… in Afghanistan I'm sending mad heroin back but not enough,"

"You said the U.S.A. was killing Black Folk?" Natasha looked at him with a quizzical expression.

"Maaaan, straight up." Joker nodded emphatically. "Look around the globe: Mogadishu, Somalia. Remember *Black Hawk Down* movie? That was the United States gettin' they ass beat cuz they Army, they whole military is full of pussies. They got whipped like Toby in ROOTS. That's Africa…Um, Saddam Hussein. The U.S. was cool wit 'im when he waged war against Iran from 1980 to 1988. Then a few years later he invades Kuwait where the U.S. has some oil wells at. 1990 to 1991 the *Gulf War* they called it. They ran him out but not before he burned all the oil wells, fires that couldn't be put out for years. Then Osama bin Laden takes out the Twin Towers. Itching for revenge the lying white honkey cock-suckers said that Saddam Hussein had WMDs (Weapons of Mass Destruction) and invaded Iraq in the Iraq War in 2003 *while* we were fighting in Afghanistan. We saw action…and it opened most of our eyes that the United States government has and always will hate Black people."

"I get it," she agreed with her brother. "You came back a different person. How many people you kill?"

"Thousands of machine gun clips, the bombs I've detonated, the grenades I've thrown, the necks I've slit with my hunting knife, the men I've beaten and tortured for information..." he trailed off while shaking and shrugging. Then he took a deep breath prior to continuing, "North Korea flies ICBMs or Inter-Continental Ballistic Missiles over Japan and they conduct nuclear bomb tests whenever the fuck they want. The fat little North Korean dictator talks mad shit to the U.S. and the U.S. don't do shit but put sanctions on the North... Look at Russia's War on Ukraine. Russia been smackin' Ukraine like a pimp slap a bitch. Russia *took* Crimea. What does the U.S. do?" Put sanctions on them. Then China spying blatantly on the United States, threatening the U.S. little ally Taiwan. Then China's record on human rights. I can line up a few others like the murder of Jamal Kashoghi by the Crown Prince. But this is my point."

He had to cough to clear his throat. Then he said: "Somalians were Blacks who fought back and wouldn't be bullied by the Americans. The U.S. *lost* that war, by people mostly in bare feet! When they brought that Blackhawk down it was embarrassing... China got a billion people and it's an economic juggernaut gaining power around the world while the U.S. dollar is bein' diminished. Plus, the U.S. is reliant on China for their rare earth elements that go inside of cell-phones, computers. The U.S. is afraid of a war with China because they have nuclear bombs, Kamikazee fighters and the U.S. would never beat them in a ground war... North

Korea has nukes and the backing of China. The U.S. has only created *hustles*-secret fuckin' jobs for everybody with a boat or a ship to smuggle in all the shit that North Korea needs. So instead of it comin' in over the radar its comin' in under the radar. Small ships, small boats, helicopters. And I'd bet it all that Russia and China is in cahoots havin' North Korea not only testin' out North Korea ICBMs and nuclear tests but Russia's and China's own ICBMs and nuclear tests-with Russian and Chinese scientists. Then last there's Russia. Why the United States ain't rollin' up in Russia like they did in *Somalia, Iraq, and Afghanistan?*" Because it's *nothin'* to these racist fuckin' bastards to shed Black and Brown blood."

"Russians are white," Natasha said.

"Exactly," he told her. Joker crossed his arms and relaxed in the comfortable chair. "I'm a different breed from ya sons and the rest of 'em. They just animal cubs. Imma be the first nigga in the hood to own a PMC."

"PMC," she repeated. "What's that?"

"Paramilitary or Private Military Corporation," he explained.

"Mercenaries," she said sighing.

"Look, Tash," he spoke in a reassuring voice. "They high school dropouts. They not ready for – and not of age for – the army… So, I'm taking all these young niggas with me before you out shopping for caskets. I already own a training facility. Government-backed."

"Where?"

. . .

"That's classified." Joker stood up. "Make a decision."

She decided to trust Joker Red.

He handed her a slip of paper. "You have a cash app?"

"I have Venmo."

He nodded. "That'll work even better."

She read the names on the paper. "Jimmie 2 Tymes, Mojo, Blood Money, Streetlyfe, Big Crip, Badman, Hop, Tip Toe, Grimm, Boom, Budda Clips, Rampage, Blue, Cocaine and Crime. More cousins, nephews and… *Rampage?* Rampage is a girl y'know?"

Joker shook his head no. "Rampage is a boy."

"Uh uh," She just looks like one. That's your second cousin, dummy. She just a butch girl."

. . .

JOKER CHUCKLED. "I'MA WHIP THEM NIGGAS ASSES. WELL… I don't care if it had a dick and a pussy between its legs!" He laughed.

NATASHA FROWNED. "THAT'S MEAN. CAN'T BELIEVE YOU DIDN'T know your own cousin was a female."

"I BARELY KNOW THEIR REAL NAMES," HE STATED WITH AN ALOOF shrug. "Just these nick names. But that's cool cuz peeps I be around go by nicknames mostly. This why no one gets all they B.I."

He used his cell phone to access his Venmo account. "Let's do this money transfer."

A COUPLE OF MINUTES LATER SHE WAS SAYING, "WOW. DAMN, bro, ten grand? Who I gotta kill?"

"NO ONE," HE TOLD HER. "JUST BE SURE ALL THEY MOMS IS ON board with me taking these niggas to training camp with me. Spread out a few hundred to each of them so they all come with basic shower shoes, cosmetics, documents, medical info, shit we need to know."

He tied off all the loose ends with her, retrieved his bag and exited with Tithi at his side.

CHAPTER TWENTY-THREE

Meth Man Ace's Ranch
Tuesday Afternoon

Joker met with remove mayonnaise and it's four living girlfriends: Blanca, Bambina, Natalya and Alexandra. All four were from the Dominican Republic and we're now prolific crystal meth manufacturers themselves.

Blanca was the clearest standout because she was not only black but had the thickest ass a man could ever hope to have, with the small waist to match. She was 5 feet 6 inches; her breasts were about the size of apples with nipples that any mammal would love. She was the oldest of the four at 28 years old.

Bambina was the petite one at 5'1", 100 pounds, very

pretty, and had hair that flowed past her tight, round, little ass. She was the best cook in the group and was currently pregnant at 25.

Natalya was a tall thick and exceptionally beautiful Dominican at 6 feet, 145 pounds. She had the most striking and piercing, blue eyes and natural blond hair. One would think she was white which was perfect because whenever Ace needed her to be White, she could turn on the "White Privilege" act. She had recently turned 23.

Alexandra was 5 feet 4 inches, 150 pounds and had bronze skin. She was in superior athletic shape and the most fun to fuck. She had no hang ups. Lex, her nickname, was not afraid to sweat or get dirty. Of the four she was the only one who liked other females from time to time. She was 26.

Ace's women were in no way like Joker's women. The Dominicana's we're all on birth control. Bambina and Ace had chosen for her to have a baby because it's what they both wanted. And in each of their several homes they never shared the same bed. The women each had their own rooms and, in some cities, their own apartments.

"There's no fuckin' way enemies ain't there, son," Joker told Ace in the privacy of Ace's home-office library. "We makin' too much money. I know them wolves is back there!"

The tall light skinned man wasn't sensing paranoia from the EIE general. "You mean *hunters*, watching and waiting for one in our flock to weaken and…"

"*Food,*" Joker nodded. "They gonna *eat*. And I *know* it, son, they want me dead. Them bombings was meant for me."

"Who did it though? And who wants you dead?" Ace questioned.

Joker cracked open a new bottle of Remy and poured himself a shot. Ace took the one he offered and they drank them at the same time.

"I don't know but it's in my dreams," Joker answered.

"You mean nightmares."

Joker nodded yes. "So what or where I think we're vulnerable is those closest to us," he surmised.

"You mean like in your own house," Meth Man said.

Joker poured them one more. "Look what A-Son and Romie did. And now this shit with Uzenna."

"Betrayal creeping closer and closer," Ace concurred. "Why not wire everything? Like a bank. They have got whole streets recorded now. Satellite pictures of our houses from space and shit. You already got a link in with them feds. Why not get your hands on the best surveillance equipment in the world?"

Joker thought that went over. I already have the Twin Towers wired up… But involving the feds? They may be too eager to do that."

"While they in bed with us?" Meth Man asked, sounding doubtful. "And risk recordin' their own dirt? Nah… Matter of fact… Who's buying all the arms for y'all?"

"Lieutenant Gates," Joker told him. "Lieutenant Sampson gates. Veteran contractor for the CIA."

. . .

"GET THE SURVEILLANCE SHIT THROUGH HIM," ACE ADVISED. "I'm talking GPS trackers, encrypted phones, spyware apps on burner phones you give out and only the best in high tech cameras."

Joker left and contacted Lt. Gates.

The Twin Towers
Chicago IL
Thursday 1:00

CHAPTER TWENTY-FOUR

The Twin Towers
Chicago IL
Thursday 1:00

Nina Overstreet was actually a very good-looking woman, with a 5 feet 9 inch tall frame and alluring curves everywhere: her ass, her long legs, her small but cute breasts and waist all held sweet chocolate treasures. She hardly ever displayed any of it, so men barely took notice. Her face was pretty, her mouth was wide, lips big – it was actually her lips that drew Joker in when he picked her up.

"Oh, my goodness," she frowned as she climbed inside of

the brand new silver Bugatti Chiron Super Sport. "Really J.R.? A Bugatti?" She scoffed.

Fortunately, she only had a small carry-on bag which she put on the floor as he drove away from O'Hare Airport. She looked around the car and had to admit, though, extremely flashy, it was a very exquisite car.

"You're the only pretty CIA agent I know, sorry," he shrugged. "Ladies aren't impressed with China anymore. Next time I'll pull out the paper plates."

That made her laugh.

"Is that a laugh *and* a smile?" Joker teased her.

She smiled. "You are nuts," she told him. "I smile."

"High-powered woman like you come through?" He said and whistled. "Nigga gotta come correct."

She looked over at him and removed her Chloë shades. "Are you flirting?"

He shrugged and smiled. "I'm just being organic. I like somethin', or someone, I'm after it. And with you… I see the cold blooded, hardened government agent with the khakis and field boots. But I also see the gentle walk and sway in them hips, and the curves of a sweet chocolate woman. Got me definitely wondering about that pussy…"

"Well, I'm not here for that," she said aloud. "And I will not be made a part of your cult."

He had to chuckle at that. "Why does everyone say that? If mine is a cult, then so is ABC's The Bachelor. And when he was alive no one called The Heff a cult leader." (Hugh Heffner)

She changed the subject. "I was sent a file from the FBI Forensic Analysis unit concerning those bomb blasts that killed your children,mothers,mothers and your comrades a few months ago. Or… Is it just 'my sweet chocolate' you want?"

His face turned to stone. "Aight. We'll go to my war room," he told her.

When they arrived, he wasted no time in heading straight to the War Room. But before he could even get inside the elevator, he was met by some of his wives and babies.

"We saw you pull up!" Brittany beamed as she held her son. "Hi, baby!"

Coral Nee was also there with their son.

Ashley held their daughter as well.

"Look at daddy's babies!" He smiled at each of them and kissed them. He also kissed and embraced each woman. "Y'all let me take care of something in the war room with Nina here and we'll all have dinner?"

The women nodded, gushing at seeing him.

"And can someone get an apartment ready for her?" He asked.

"I'll get it," Coral volunteered.

"Send me Leah, please!" He led Nina to the staircase and they walked up to the floor the war room was on.

"How many you have now?" Nina teased him.

"Louise, Melodie, Diane, Julia, Romie… Uzenna," he trailed off. "They all gone… so, eight."

Nina was certainly curious about him. There was a power and attraction about him that was causing her to like him even more despite all he had going on.

"Hey, Daddy," Leah said, excited, as she rushed through the front door just moments after they settled down in front of the large wall TV screens.

"Nice," Nina complimented them on the war room's digital communications equipment. She was impressed.

Leah had her arms wrapped around his neck as he took the time to kiss and hold her. Leah was not that tall at 5'6, 140 pounds. Her hair had been dyed a bleached blonde which brought out her pretty blue eyes and small round face. And though she had lost the baby weight she's still maintained that delectable southern ass and thighs he loved so much.

"Leah is a godsend" Joker told Nina as he palmed her rear and urged her on towards Nina. "Not only is she from the south doesn't she have the sweetest girl-next-door-accent?"

"Joker Red, you're embarrassing me!" Leah said and covered her mouth real quick because she'd let the deep southern drawl be heard.

Nina had to smile. "She is lovely," Nina warmed up inside, liking Leah instantly. She was so girly girl it was just too cute.

"I'm good. I just freaked out, man," she said.

"Aight," he said as she sat down. "This is chemical and signature analysis…"

Nina handed her the electronic flash drive which held the information she wanted to share with him. Leah took it and plugged it into the USB connection. "Uploading…"

She sat down and turned on the 86-inch TV first. Then she turned on a smaller 32-inch which is what they were looking at as the file uploaded.

"Why's *Frank Brown Analysis I'* appear… His name appears quite a few times?" Joker was standing behind Leah to her right. "He's not part of-"

"Oh my god," Leah muttered. "I see what this is. It's about the Hummer dealership bombings."

"Yeah," Joker said. "What we got? Who da fuck did it bae so I can murda everything. I mean blood everywhere."

"I know, Daddy," Leah said, reading.

"From the analysis reports…" Nina stated. "The Bureau wanted to rule out these devices being made by one of our own people. They, the FBI, got a hold of EIE service records to see who had knowledge of bomb making. One by one they were profiled and then fit the profile. Not even the late Frank Brown."

"Ghostman neither?" Joker questioned her.

"Ghostman Dinero?" Leah asked surprised.

"No one inside of EIE," Nina said empathetically.

He was biting the skin near his thumbnail as he read through the FBI file. Leah was right there with him-reading along obsessively almost. She clicked on to the "crime scene photographs" and she suddenly lost it. She went into hysterics. That's how painful it was for her.

"Louise! Julia! Oh, god!" She screamed holding her midsection as if it were her entire soul. *"Diane! Mel!"* She yelled, her voice a piercing cry.

Her anguish took Nina by surprise.

"God dammit! He shut the images off and turned to Leah with tears in his eyes. "Hey, baby want me to call the girls?" He asked, wanting to calm her down.

She ran to the bathroom, vomiting along the way.

"She's traumatized," Nina said, following her. "Let me…"

He returned to the file and skipped past the photos. He read a report entitled *"Signature Analysis"* and another marked *"Chemical Analysis."* Leah returned. She was okay. Trembling but steady.

"You good, mama?" He asked, kissing her cheek. "This shit is hard."

"Okay," she said, reading it.

"Blow that report up, babe," he ordered.

She blew it up.

"Put it on the big screen." He sat back, twirling a pen in his hand. "It identifies two types of C-4, two bombs. Each packed with nails, nuts, bolts and ball bearings. Click on 'Conclusion.'"

She clicked on 'Conclusion.'

"Blow it up; Put it up on the big screen."

She followed his orders.

He stood in front of the 86-inch wall screen reading it carefully. "Slick, sly FBI and ATF and CIA travel the world seekin' out and collectin' data on every bomb that goes off… But they lack the eyes of a criminal."

Nina stood alongside him. "The report is inconclusive. What do *you* see?" She asked, searching his face for answers.

"They looked for all the missin' fuckin' video and it's all scrubbed," he mentioned. "A nigga spits on the *sidewalk* it's on camera or on the Cloud or something! Who has the money to make that happen?

"Or the *power*," Nina threw it out there.

"And right *here*," Joker said, moving closer to the big screen. "They say *'these devices contained nails, nuts, bolts and ball bearings. Global data collected shows this particular combination has occurred in 43 events over the past ten years. However, in this particular event the exact brand of ball has only occurred in this combination six times in 10 years.'* And they list in which countries those ball bearings were used."

Israel.

United States.

Yemen.

London.

Lebanon.

And *Albania*.

"Ok," Joker said. "We learned a lot here today. Who's hungry?"

Leah got up.

"You go ahead, baby," Joker told her. "Nina and I need to talk. You hush up about what you saw ya heard?"

"Heard nothin'."

"Good girl." He turned to Nina when Leah exited the apartment.

"That bomb was meant for me," Joker pointed at the screen. "Them fuckers killed my boys, my women, three of my daughters and one of my sons. And I'm in a blind rage."

"I can tell," she acknowledged, reaching out to wipe away tears he didn't even know were there. "You have someone in mind?"

"My Indian girl just got a new tattoo," he revealed. "I noticed it at the funeral after party in New York. She's so innocent and naïve. I asked her who did it. She told me Honey B recommended some Albanian to do it."

Nina's eyes shifted over to the list frozen on the screen. "Albania is on the bottom. And you think that's too coincidental?"

He nodded and filled her in about Honey B's origins in the organization.

Nina thought about it afterward. "We have to probe deeper into her affairs and her contacts south of the border. Let's follow the money. Expand the probe into Ghostman's affairs because she's his woman and pregnant with this child. In doing all this listening in on the phone conversations she's having with the cartel contacts, etcetera, we're sure to learn something and pray that it's good news. That they ain't involved."

"Let's go eat," he told her.

She followed him out.

The Twin Towers
Friday Morning

CHAPTER TWENTY-FIVE

The Twin Towers
Friday Morning

Lieutenant Sampson gates was a former U.S. Army Ranger infantry who fought in *Enduring Freedom, Iraqi Freedom* and the *Somalian war*. He was first Battalion, Seventy-Fifth Regiment, Hunter Army Airfield. He was 42 years old, a tall imposing figure, ruggedly handsome and made his home in the jungles of Costa Rica unless a great paycheck came calling.

"Overstreet," he acknowledged her as he stepped out of the white van he rented at Midway Airport.

"Lieutenant," she said, shaking his hand.

"What do y'all need from me?" Joker inquired as he stood

on the sidewalk in front of the Twin Towers.

"This won't be an overnight job," Overstreet told Joker. "The first thing you need to do is gather up everyone in your organization and require them to carry the encrypted cell phones. That's most important."

Lt. Gates nodded. "A delivery vehicle should be here sometime this afternoon with those devices. Number two. I am having several tech teams install the very best in hi-tech security cameras inside and outside each and every establishment you use to create income. This includes houses, apartments... Even getting someone inside of Ghostman's mansion."

"Good luck with that," Joker said doubtfully.

"At the very least we'll put trackers on his and Honey B's vehicles," Overstreet said. "This will be a very elaborate, sophisticated, well thought out operation. Babies were bombed and we are very interested in uncovering the conspiracy here. You are an asset to us, and you don't mind footing the bill right?"

"Hell no," Joker said, texting Leah.

Moments later she came out pulling two suitcases on a four-wheel cart.

"Ditch that rental," Joker told them. "Take one of mine. Take the bulletproof, bomb proof, Escalade or one of those Range Rovers."

"How about that two-million-dollar Bugatti," Nina said humorously, pointing at it.

"Two mill?" Joker laughed. "I wish."

"Is that the Chiron Super Sport?" Gates asked him.

Joker nodded.

Lt. Gates whistled. "Yeah. She's more than two million. More like four million."

"Exactly," Joker nodded. Only five hundred made. 1600 horsepower, 273 mph. It has large turbo changes and highly efficient compressor wheels that cause the seven-gear dual-clutch transmission to shift from sixth to seventh gear at 250 mph even at full load. Hands down it's the baddest car on the planet."

"The cops will stop you just to look at it," Nina said. "Or give you a speeding ticket."

"I'll just throw the fine money out the fuckin' window," Joker stated. "At 273 mph? I'll be a blur to them!" He laughed.

"We'll take the black Range Rover," Nina told Leah who stood by laughing. "What?" the tough CIA agent stated.

"You got him talking about that Bugatti," Leah said. "Nobody here wants to even drive in there cuz it's too fast! I'm scared to get in it."

"That's cuz you a little squirrel," he told her as he walked over to load the suitcases full of cash into the Range Rover.

"Aye, L-T," Nina was saying to Gates. "There's 4 million in these cases, just like you asked. And inside one of them is a complete file of his entire network."

Joker returned.

"Every car every place of business, every employee, business contact down to the cleaning lady," Nina ordered. "There's a lot of strippers in these clubs he owns throughout Meth Alley."

"And a lot of clubs," Joker added. I can't watch all of them. There's forty-eight at last count..."

"In a month you'll be able to," Gates promised. "This location will be your central intelligence network?"

Nina shook her head no.

"Yeah, I agree with her," Joker stated. "Too many eyes. Lease a safe house and make it the CIN."

Gates and Nina set out to handle the massive task while Joker waited for the shipment of encrypted phones to be delivered.

"Hey, Lee?"

She had a power washer that she was using to wash away dirt and debris from the Twin Tower One cement walkway with.

"I need a big, big, favor," he stated.

"I need one, too, she countered.

"We're going to be calling in every employee of EIE in groups of ten to twenty," he told her. "I want them here face to face for the new encrypted cell phones I'll be giving them."

"Why don't you just mail them?"

"Just do what I tell you," he said.

"Okay." She turned off the water. "Now my turn. I need a big, big, favor."

"What's that?"

"I need to be fucked," She emphasized with a shy grin.

"I like how you act all shy when you say that," he laughed, taking her hand and pulling her inside. "Where we goin'? We go upstairs they gonna be all over me."

"C'mon. to the war room," she said mischievously.

CHAPTER TWENTY-SIX

The Pendry Manhattan West
Friday Afternoon

Uzenna had returned to the United states after being denied permanent citizenship status in Belize. She was able to withdraw nearly $100k from an account that she kept there. She exhausted every avenue that she could in order to obtain citizenship, but she lacked proper documentation.

She spent several consecutive days, for hours at a time, at the US embassy but their assistance only went but so far. For instance, to apply for temporary citizenship she needed a birth certificate and Social Security card. The Social Security Administration was asking her to show up in person because there seemed to be an issue with her maiden name and current name. She was so frustrated but in order to become a permanent resident in Belize she was first required to live there for at least one year. To do that she first needed to be granted temporary citizenship, but her documents were not in proper order.

When she arrived at New York's La Guardia Airport she was processed through U.S. customs and asked to wait while her luggage was searched for contraband.

And hour later she was released and sent on her way. She wondered why it had taken so long. She was ultimately whisked away with her son in an Uber car she was able to flag down as soon as she exited the American Airlines terminal.

"Can you recommend a nice hotel in Manhattan?" She asked a female driver.

"I'm hearing so much about the new Pendry Manhattan West," the white woman, who was in her fifties, suggested. "The Pendry is big out in California. They're not cheap though."

"Okay. To the Pendry please."

Thirty minutes later they were in front of the majestic Pendry Manhattan West in Midtown. Uzenna's luggage was immediately carted inside by a short Kevin Hart-looking Black man who was one of the many bellboys there. Employee or not she kept a sharp eye on her suitcases because she had bought new things for her and Baby Joker.

"Credit card ma'am?" The cashier asked at the registration desk.

"I lost all of my cards, but I have cash and a passport," she offered.

Hotels like the one she was at particularly frowned on cash deposits unless a security deposit came with it.

"Let me call my mana-" the raven-haired college aged cashier started.

Uzenna cut her off. "No need. I have a decent security deposit. How much is one night?"

"Five hundred and five dollars," the girl informed Uzenna. "And it's just you and the cutie there?"

Uzenna smiled as the hotel manager walked past and stopped to observe after seeing the cash.

"I need at least three days," she explained and handed over a stack of cash. "Five grand okay for now? I'll collect the security on checkout."

The cashier looked at the manager and the manager nodded.

Uzenna was escorted to her 17th floor room by the bellboy. He brought her luggage in as she walked over to the floor-to-ceiling windows that looked out over the skyline. She looked around at the honey-hued wood and all the beautiful potted plants.

"Hey," Uzenna handed the bellboy a $20 bill. "Do they have spicy baked chicken, vegetables and rice in the kitchen?"

"Yes ma'am," he answered. "Call them and ask for anything on the menu. It pops up on the TV or computer. Just click on *Food Service Menu* order what you want, and they'll deliver it."

He left and she ordered food. She examined the menu and they had everything she needed. Baby food and much more. How convenient. She put on *Cadillac Records*, one of her favorite movies. She paused it to shower and bathe Baby Joker first.

The food arrived and she immediately dug in as she watched the movie. Baby Joker was only six months old, but he was a big, healthy, six months. He noticed her eating and he reached for her mouth. She tried to put him on her nipple, but he snatched his little face away.

"What man don't want titties?" She cooed at him, but he wasn't having it. She used one of his baby spoons to feed him mashed potatoes and gravy from her plate. She chewed up small bits of the baked chicken and fed that to him as well. He had a look of delight on his face at his first taste of meat.

"Damn, boy!" She was laughing as he flailed his arms around, all excited. "You want real food now huh?"

Later he fell asleep next to her as she watched *Cadillac Records*. Her favorite part of the movie was when Etta James (played by the great Beyoncé Knowles-Carter) went into the hotel bathroom and belted out the classic *All I Could Do Was Cry*. And that's exactly what Uzenna did.

She was homesick, depressed, afraid and isolated in the world all alone. So much tragedy, despair and death. Romie, Louise and her daughter Stefanie, Melodie and her son Justin, Diane and her daughter Francesca, and Julia and her daughter Afton.

Just to think of them now made Uzenna tremble and shake from the enormous sobs that consumed her body. And hearing Beyoncé sing Etta James' *"I'd Rather Be Blind"* only served to blast all of Etta's pain into her own. Women were just wired like that. Sister to sister. Woman to woman.

Uzenna so wished she would've had a different life. A decent mother who would have protected her and not allowed her daughters to be subjected to such a shameful and evil father and grandfather. Her mother had turned a blind eye and each tender aged Moses sister had had to submit to their incestuous molestation and rapes for an extended period of time.

As *Cadillac Records* credits rolled, she thought about The Mafia Massacre and how her murderous husband and his band of hittaz had bombed the place. They killed a lot of people that night and it felt good to have a hero.

But we also have blood on our hands, Uzenna thought to herself as she put on some country music. If she played DaBaby or Cardi B like she wanted to Baby Joker would wake up dancing to that shit. So she put on Darius Walker from the band Hootie & The Blowfish.

She missed Joker Red and wished she could take back what she'd said. The pain she caused him had come from her own pain and fear.

Monk, Black N9NE, Big Chief, Fast Eddie, Mustafa, Ground War, she thought about them, feeling horrified that they were dead, and she had said all of what she did. *And to put the icing on the cake — and salt in the womb — I had absolutely no regard for what Iani texted me about the losses of Bonecrusher and Knarf.* She picked up her phone…

She texted Joker: *Daddy, I'm so very sorry about not being at the funeral services. The pain and sorrow would have been too great to sit through for me anyway because Monk, N9NE, Chief, Eddie, Mustafa, Ground War, Bone and Knarf were all my Big Brothers. I'm sorry that my mental health, all the losses, I had COVID-19 at the time, and raising all these babies... I said some words I wish very badly I could take them back. But I can't. Knowing that and taking into account the type of man you are, I ran. I'm afraid for my life. Anyways, we are safe. We have money. And for what it's worth I'm still your wife and I love you. But I no longer feel like #1 or felt like #1 I mean. Out here it's OK being #2 because junior is number one. Love always, Zen.*

She read the letter carefully.

Then she pressed "send."

CHAPTER TWENTY-SEVEN

Brittani Dane's Apartment
The Twin Towers
Friday 3:55 PM

"C'mere you!" Joker grabbed Brittani Dane, his red head sister-wife, and carried her out of the Jacuzzi and into the bedroom. They were both nude except for the thong undies she still had on.

Brittani never lost her baby weight and Joker encouraged her not to even try because she was hot as hell at 160 pounds, 5 feet 5 inches, with the most exotic tattoos on her body. She had the most perfect picture of Joker's face done on her neck behind her left ear. She had long tresses of red hair for days but whenever she put it in a ponytail or an up-do his photo could be clearly seen.

She had three more tattoos with his name on her: one on her ass, one above the pubic line of her pussy and one on her foot. She had some soft and pretty feet, too. It never failed with him. If they were fresh out of the water Joker would suck her toes and that was something she looked forward to. Nothing made her wetter than having her toes sucked.

He pulled her thong panties off and kissed her deeply, meaningfully. "I'm so sorry, baby. You know I love you right?" He stared into her pretty eyes.

She nodded, her pussy dripping juices already.

"I know. I love you, too," she assured him. "You my Daddy, my husband, my man. I love you. Don't be sorry for handlin' yours. You a warrior."

He sucked on her protruding nipples as she gyrated her wide hips, rubbing her empty pussy against his quadricep. He wanted to bite on and suck them warm creamy titties all day.

"You still got milk in 'em," he whispered. "I love the sweet taste of that milk."

"That's your creation," she whispered. "You created the life of our son Baby Joker/David Three. You did that with that big black dick...and that strong seed you have in them juicy balk. Umm, baby!"

Never failed with him. He was sucking on her pretty painted toes. She cocked her legs open and ran her middle finger slowly over her moist petals to wet it real good. She sloshed it all around inside of her small wet opening, and twirled it all over her labia, down over her perineum and around and around her anal orifice. He watched and his manhood grew to a stiff angry looking weapon with veins pulsating all over it.

He put all five of her toes into his mouth at the same time and she moaned loudly as his tongue raked across them. He loved her small feet. He went back and forth between them kissing her ankles, loving the tattoo with his name on her left foot. He sliced his tongue in between each toe making that pussy wetter. She was cumming every few minutes, pinching her clit with one hand while the other hand was able to slide a finger inside of her asshole from beneath.

"You still my nasty slut, baby?"

"You already know." She was whining and writhing all crazy, turned all the way on. "I'm your slutty white girl."

"I can smell your slutty pussy."

"*Unnnhh, baby!*" she whined through a mini orgasm. "I *need* you to smell it so you can have your meal. Come eat, baby. Come eat mommy's slutty white pussy."

He couldn't hold back. He couldn't lay on his stomach because his penis was too aroused, too big. So he lay slightly to his side and looked at her excited seam. Her clitoris looked like it was thumping and begging to be sucked, licked, bit and pinched. He stuck his nose up against her clit and used his thumbs to pry her dark pink petals apart. He ran his nose up and down each side of her soaked contours, sniffing and smelling and savoring one of his delicious women.

"You love white girls, huh, Daddy? You love our scent.

How our white skin contrasts with yours. How tight our little pussies are. Smell that pussy, Daddy! OHHH, SHHIITTT!!"

He had latched onto her clitoris and went to work. He knew she had to have a lot of clitoral stimulation and attention paid to the upper left portion of her clit to make her nut. But he also had other plans for her hot ass. He slid a thumb deep inside of her anus with his right hand and he thrust three fingers from his left hand inside of her pussy. She was covered with a glistening sheen of sweat by now. She had her hands on her breasts, twisting and squeezing her extended nipples which were lubricated with the baby milk.

He was greedily sucking on her clitoris and every now and then he'd stop to lap up her cum which she had plenty of.

"You're a fuckin' honeypot!" he proclaimed. "A beehive full of honey!"

He got on top of her and eased his enormous monster dick inside of her tight squeezing pussy. He grabbed her hair, making her look at him, at his dick.

"Watch that shit go in and out," he commanded her. "You damn right I love white girls! See how hard you make me?"

"OOOOOOO, yesss, Daddy! I see it," she cried as he pounded her into the mattress. "Don't stop fuckin' me! I can feel you in my belly button! Fuck me, Joker!! Fuck this white girl! Fuck my slutty white pussy!"

Damn she made that shit sound sexy, he thought.

"This pussy feel brand new, baby," he said as he slowed down and made love to her now. She liked the rough stuff but when he did it like this, he knew he was locking in the emotional connection they both needed. "I love you, babe. I truly do."

"Oh my god," she moaned as he grinded deeper and deeper until that second vaginal cavity of hers popped open and let him in. She screamed and burst like a water balloon. *"AAAIIIEEE!!!* OHHHHH, Daddy!!! I love you!!"

It felt like she'd peed but it was clear and syrupy Bartholin Gland Fluids. When she did that he pounded hard with his entire ten gliding in and out until his seed gushed out in five big spurts.

"CUUUMMMIIINNNGGG!" One loud, drawn out, cry and his sweaty body seized and quaked through a momentous orgasm.

They held tightly onto each other, kissing and caressing, perspiration pooling between them.

"White girls are the best," he declared. "Y'all are loyal. Submissive, Youse listen. No bullshit. And when a nigga down in prison y'all bitches ride."

Brittani grinned. "That's us," she agreed.

"You on birth control?" he asked.

She had her face all up in his armpit. "No. Why would I do that? You want me to?"

"Hell no. But the last time you and I made love-and your dam broke like *that*-David Three was on the way."

She shrugged. "I like bein' a mom. I love bein' your wife and livin' in a commune. So we need for nothin'. I'm proud of this government stuff you're doin' even though it's dangerous. I wish the drug stuff can disappear because it scares us... Now."

"Now?"

"The babies," she said, reading his face.

"Speakin' of which," he said, kissing her forehead. "I been thinkin' of somethin'. Let's shower, change these sheets out and get everyone to my penthouse. Family meetin'."

That's when he checked his phone and saw a text from a private number. He looked at the first few words in the text and knew it was Uzenna...

CHAPTER TWENTY-EIGHT

Joker's Penthouse

Friday 5:30 PM

All the girls showed up, including Tithi who had just come from work. Coral, Ashley, Leah, Eden, Valerie, Iani, Brittani and Tithi all were seated in the living room of Joker's penthouse.

"How much you wanna bet he *knows*," Brittani challenged Iani.

"What, that he can't remember all thirteen babies names?" Ashley blurted, wanting in on the bet.

"No. She's sayin' he *can* remember," Iani corrected her. "C-A-N. He can. I got fifty sayin' he messes up at least one."

Tithi was amused. "You think he'll forget his own children name?" she asked.

"I got the fifty," Ashley pulled out some cash. "I'm against you Iani. He'll remember."

"I got fifty against Iani," Brittani said. "Who else says he can't remember all thirteen?"

Leah, Eden, Valerie and Coral said he'd forget at least one name.

"What are you bitches up to?" he asked as he walked into the room and sat with a large bag between his legs.

Tithi explained and he smirked at her afterward.

He smiled. "Who's against me?" he dared them.

"Iani, Lee, Val, Coral and Eden," Ashley informed him.

"I'm bettin' fifty on myself," he told them. "Who want it?" he pulled out some money.

"I'll do it," Tithi said. "You'll mess up one at least." This was so amusing.

"Name the mother of the baby, too," Iani said quickly.

He cleared his throat. "I'm doing' those still here first and the others at the end."

The girls agreed on that.

"Coral-Bradford; Ashley-Sonja; Lee-David Two; Brittani-David Three; he paused to look at Iani." Iani-Rose; Valerie-Ivory Brown; Eden-Eve; Uzenna-David One; Romie-King Mundo who still here…Louise Stefanie…Melodie-Justin…Diane-Francesca…Julia-Afton; Tithi…is ten weeks."

"What?!" Ashley gasped, looking at Tithi. "So cool! Now you're one of us!"

"Congratulations!" Leah beamed as did the other women.

During that melee Joker received another text. This one from Nina Overstreet: *Our girl was in Belize City and visited the U.S. Embassy Passport/Documents Office several times...she re-entered the country and held her based on a red flag notice I'd entered when we saw that she'd left which you were told about. Now she's held up in a Midtown hotel named "The Pandry Manhattan West." I asked an investigator to watch her until further notice.*

"Aight," he said as the bets were settled and the women settled down. He opened up the bag and passed out the brand-new encrypted phones. "Everybody get your old phones and give them to Leah."

"I *like* my phone," Ashley complained.

"They've been compromised so turn them over," he said. "No arguments."

They all left to retrieve their phones. Those who needed time to copy down information they had stored there were granted it.

"Wow these are niiiice," Iani stated as she turned her new phone on.

"Next thing," he said, Uzenna on his mind making his mood cold. "We movin' into a gated community outside of Chicago."

"Aw man!" Iani scoffed. "I'm tired of movin'."

He took a deep breath. "Y'all wanna be blown to bits too?"

Silence all around.

"I'm supposed to be your protector," he reminded them.

"And do y'all like the checks you receive now from Indian Sun Condos via Air BNB?"

They all nodded.

"Well," he shrugged. "We can make money hands over fist off of this place…if we move out of it. We own it."

The women softened.

"There's a cul-de-sac inside of this brand-new gated community I been keepin' my eyes on," he revealed to them. "There's ten houses lining both sides of the street going down into the cul-de-sac. I want to buy all ten houses and build our-"

Brittani raised her hand. "So each of us have our own home?"

"In your name and the name of our first born," Joker nodded. "No one here wants all these cryin' kids bunched under one roof."

Brittani shook her head. "Then how bout buyin' the *land* and building us each a house we can have customed how we like?"

He sat back, "I was thinkin' of somethin' more immediate. The threat is knockin'."

"We can move anywhere, Daddy," Valerie, the tall bombshell said. "We don't have toIllinois,llinois do we? We're not runnin' TPP-2 like we thought…"

"Cuz narco paper can be sent from anywhere to tell you the truth," Little Eden piped up.

"We don't *need* to be here in Illinois," he told them. "It's just convenient for *me* to be. Where y'all wanna go? Back to New York?"

"Miami," one said.

"Fort Lauderdale," another said.

"Miami Beach," one more said.

"Fort Lauderdale," someone else said.

"We're talkin' *property*," Brittani urged as different women said different things.

Joker looked at his phone. "The two are barely even forty miles apart. And Fort Lauderdale is mansions and yachts while Miami is boats and houses."

"You got the money, big dog!" Leah said, tucking her right leg underneath her and giggling.

Joker looked at her. "You high?"

"A little smokey." She smiled.

"Aight," he stood up, kissing Leah first then the rest. "Tithi, you got any objections to Florida?"

"No its *warm* there!" she said standing on her tip toes to kiss him. "Like in my country."

"Cool," he said. "Y'all recon where you wanna be as long as we can gate it and secure y'all and the kids. So, get us the land. Can we have and fly a helicopter in and out? In the meantime, find the ideal place to move ASAP. Now. Yesterday. I want us outta here."

"In Florida, while we're there," Iani said, wanting to make sure.

Joker was getting annoyed. "What does *ASAP. NOW.* And *yesterday* mean? You shouldn't wait till you get there. Find us *nine* houses in a gated community before youse even leave and lease them. Nine houses all back-to-back, next to each other."

"Okay," Iani responded meekly.

"Don't be like that," he said. "C'mere. All y'all…"

They all group hugged.

Joker took off in his Bugatti and headed to the airport where, fortunately, he already had a charter jet ready to go. While he had been sitting and talking to the girls, he'd used Lisa Kiefer Sayer's JETASAP.com app and all he had to do now was get to Chicago Midway and he'd be on his way to New York.

An hour and fifteen minutes later he was strapped into his seat as the sleek new jet was climbing to 30,000 feet across the darkening Chicago skies.

CHAPTER TWENTY-NINE

The Pandry Manhattan West

Midnight – Friday

The charcoal gray Mercedes-Benz sprinter limousine pulled up to a stop and Joker looked up at the hotel. He sent a text to Nina and told her to order her investigator to stand down.

"You in the city??" She texted back.

"Affirmative."

He spoke to the driver. "Don't move alright?"

"You're my supervisor for…" He glanced at the digital clock on the dashboard, "seven more hours."

Joker walked into the hotel dressed like he was in a GQ photo or something. He wore a tan Armani suit, Versace

Gators on his feet, white shirt and black tie. He scanned the lobby and noticed several busy bellboys and one slender, very pretty white girl at the registration desk with raven hair.

He approached her, removed his shades and smiled. She wore the Star of David emblem on a silver chain around her neck. He calculated rather or not she could be bribed. *Shiid,* he thought, *she a Jew bitch. Jews is the greediest mufuckas on this earth.* She did return a smile, too. So so, Joker went for it.

"Question for the pretty girl," Joker said warmly.

She smiled brightly for him. "How may I help you?"

"How much does a cashier make here?" he questioned.

"I'm a student so I'm at the bottom," she replied with her hands moving more than her mouth. "Ten an hour."

He pulled out a stack of $100 bills and piled off five of them. She opened her mouth to say something but stopped.

"You wanna make five hundred in sixty seconds?" He asked her.

"I, um, sure." She looked curious.

"First, so you're 100% comfortable here's my ID," he stated and pulled out his military identification.

"Sergeant David Leon Hodges," she read the ID. "U.S. Army Ranger. Wow. Thank you for your service."

He nodded. "You're worth it."

"Aww," she touched her hand to her chest.

"My wife and child checked in here," he said to her. "What room are they in?"

"I'm…" She hesitated. "Oh, god, I can get in trouble if she complains."

"One thousand dollars." He pushed the $1000 towards her.

She snatched up the money. "What the hell. Hold on. Her name?"

"Uzenna Hodges," he informed her. "U-Z-E-"

"Room 1705," she revealed, cutting him off.

"Gimme a keycard," Joker asked her.

"No way. I already g-"

He peeled off another thousand and handed it to her. "A thousand more?"

"Are you gonna hurt them?" She was nervous.

"Never. Promise." He removed his shades. "Trust me. You have my name."

She took the cash and gave him the room card. He walked away and got onto the elevator. He got off on the 17th floor and found her room.

UZENNA HAD DONE SO MUCH RUNNING AROUND EARLIER IN THE day that after bathing and eating with Baby Joker she'd fallen asleep with him still awake next to her. Something jarred her out of her sleep, and she knew right away that it was her full bladder. She dashed into the bathroom and peed like a pony. She drank a glass full of water and re- entered the dark room. She looked for Baby Joker on the bed and he wasn't there!

Just then the light in the furthest corner of the room popped on and Uzenna screamed. There, Joker stood with his happy son in his arms. The baby was clearly tired, his head laying against his father's chest, but he was delighted to see Joker. Uzenna noticed the dirty diaper the baby had been wearing had been discarded on top of the dresser and he was now not only freshly changed but fully dressed. Joker only stared her down with a scowl on his face. She stood frozen at first but, robotically, she started packing up everything. She knew, somehow, that he wouldn't hurt her.

The time seemed to stand still but it wasn't. Joker went out in the hallway and waited because while she was packing, she had on those sky-blue lace booty shorts that rode all the way up in her a asscrack and her love lips were showing out the edges from the back when she leaned or bent over the suitcase to pack. Females always thought they could use the sex weapon in any situation. They could be pistol whipped and ready to die for some shiesty shit they did and – with blood dripping out their mouth – crack open them legs and show a nigga that pussy puff. Thing is, even the most hardened killers fall for that shit, giving a bitch one more opportunity to fuck the nigga over.

Joker wasn't beat for that goofy shit… She sat all four suitcases out in the hallway, and he walked off without picking up one of them for her. He went down the elevator after waiting for her to load all four of the heavy pieces onto the elevator car. Luckily for her a bellboy saw what was going on when they got on the ground floor. He grabbed a nearby cart while she went to the desk and retrieved her security deposit and the unused money where the extra day paid for.

She got inside the Mercedes-Benz Sprinter after tipping the bellboy. Joker ordered the driver to take them to Kennedy

Airport. He cradled his son in his arms, and she saw him kissing and smelling the infant as he slept.

An hour later they were inside of the charter jet, it's engine screaming as it sliced through the dark skies heading West. All throughout the entire thing, joker never uttered a word to her.

Uzenna held Baby Joker as Joker drove them to the Twin Towers. It was nearly 6:00 AM when they arrived. Joker noticed Bible Reed standing out in front of the building and Joker walked slowly up to him.

"Hallelujah," Bible said proudly. "God protected your family."

Joker inhaled and exhaled deeper than he ever did, emotion in his eyes.

Uzenna watched Joker go inside and looked up at Bible Reed. "He hates me now," she said.

Bible looked scary standing there. "Jesus said the good shepherd can have 100 sheep out to pasture but even if one gets lost, he goes and finds that one sheep... Leaving the other 99 behind..."

"Damn." She was stuck, tears welling in her eyes.

"Where were you?" Bible asked.

She wiped her tears. "He came to New York unexpectedly. I woke up to him at my hotel."

"A man like that doesn't go through all that from hate, child," Bible wisely stated. "Unless it meant a bullet in your head. You're that one lost sheep. All of us here are the 99."

She nodded, leaned up as far as she could and kissed Bible's cheek. "That means so much, Bible."

"Hee, hee, hee," he chuckled, bashful.

Inside, all of the women were at his bedroom door.

"Uzenna!!" Iani instantly yelped with surprise and ran to hug her younger sister. Each of the girls got their chance to embrace and kiss Uzenna. Iani was shaking. "What's wrong?" Uzenna pointed at the door.

"He sobbing!" Leah said, tears streaming down her face. "We thought something bad happened!"

Uzenna heard his painful wails, and her stomach was in knots. Joker was a man with a lot of demons, in a lot of pain.

"My work is cut out for me," she said feeling completely overwhelmed and exhausted. "I need all of y'all to rally up. Take my baby and leave me alone with him."

"Wait, wait," Iani stopped her. "Tell us *everything* so we ain't blind bats here. *What happened?*"

Uzenna told them how she went to Mississippi, and then to Belize because she had less money in the U.S. bank than she thought. She ran it all down to them. All the way to the present moment.

"*Manhattan?*" Leah said more than asked. "He was sitting here last evening giving us encrypted phones! Saying we were under threat, and we moved into a secure community here in Illinois."

"But we talked him into Florida," Ashley added telling her all the details.

Iani was baffled. "He did get a text but said nothing about going to New York! They were on you, man. He used the FBI or CIA to locate you. He probably knew the whole time where you was. That man love you and his kids. His first-born, too? Man… Yeah, yo work's cut out. C'mon y'all."

"Yeah, I'm going back to bed," Valerie said. "You have a lot of dick-suckin' and cum, swallowin' to do."

"Not funny," Uzenna said and saw all of the girls out.

Tithi stayed.

"Everybody else left," Uzenna told her.

"That's them," Tithi shrugged. "Not me."

"I need space with him," Uzenna explained.

"You have it," Tithi said, walking into one of the several spare rooms and slamming the door shut and locking it. Uzenna stared at the door, her mouth open in shock. "No this bitch didn't."

CHAPTER THIRTY

Ghostman's Mansion
Saturday 10:00 AM

"Apolina, wait, baby!" Honey B reached for the 5-foot 2 inch little Panamanian hottie but Apolina avoided her grasp and hopped out of the bed.

However, Ghostman was walking out of the bathroom and stopped her. "Where you goin'? "he asked with a lewd smile on his face.

"Papi, my asshole and my pussy is raw, she argued in a whine. "I can't. They need time to rest."

"What about, your lips?" he asked. "Nothin' wrong with those."

Apolina scoffed and brushed past him to go to the bathroom. "My lips are puffy and sore from you fucking my face this morning. Don't y'all ever quit?"

"How you the granddaughter of the late great Manuel Noriega and you in here tappin' out?" Ghostman teased her. "From *pleasure*."

Ghostman made love to his 23-year-old half Mexicana, half Puerto Rican wife before she went crazy from the horny state Apolina had left her in moments ago. They'd actually been at it since last night but they we're all on "ecstasy" pills and percocet so Ghostman had "Dope Balls" – he couldn't cum, which prolonged the sex.

When Ghostman and Honey B were finally finished Apolina was back in their immaculately furnished master bedroom wearing a translucent black satin robe, fresh out of the shower.

"And FYI, *Ghostman Dinero*," Apolina said sarcastically. "I'm not, Manuel Noriega's granddaughter. I'm his great granddaughter. And wasn't nobody tappin' out."

Ghostman, breathing hard, turned to observe her as she braided her long Pocahontas-style braid back. "Okay, smart ass … but call it what it was – you tappin out."

"Damn I like her so much!" Honey B said as she crawled on all fours to the edge of the bed and lay on her belly with her legs crossed." "C'mere, Miss Noriega. Kiss ya mama."

Apolina smiled and came to her. They kissed deeper than two women should ever be kissing. Ghostman lit up a stick of purple haze and smiled.

"How long that lil pussy needs to rest?" Honey B inquired.

"For you? Tomorrow," Apolina purred as they feather kissed each other. "For your husband's big D? Two days. Apolina's cellphone went off and she grabbed it read text. "Hmph," she said. "I'm being summoned to EIE HQ. I have to bring this Phone. What the hell, man!" She sighed.

Honey B got up and read the text. "You know anything about this?" She asked Ghostman, shoving the phone at him.

"I have no idea," he said. "I don't go down there 'less I have to. Apolina is

Girls, is on EIE payroll. She ain't one of Valoria's girls."

"It has to be more to it than exchanging cellphones, "Honey B concluded. "Get dressed and head on to EIE HQ. Take his pride and joy Bugatti."

Ghostman nodded. "Yeah. If you take that I'll take one of your tits off ya chest."

"Oh, shit, Daddy, I got one, too," Honey B stated with a frown. "Check your phone."

Ghostman looked around for his phone and finally found it on the shelf inside of his closet. *"Son, we got a shipment of encrypted phones. We need to REQUIRE every breathing soul in the EIE organization to have one. This way all communication is protected and all currency can be sent through the proper chan-nels,"* he read the entire text aloud.

Honey B looked at him. He looked back at her. And Apolina glanced at both of them.

"Shiiid, we all gotta go," Ghostman shrugged. "If we

don't what'll that look like? He has encrypted phones for us. Not the first phones he's given us.

"Right." Honey B went to shower and they all got dressed.

An hour later they climbed into Ghostman's Cadilac Escalade and headed to the Twin Towers.

CHAPTER THIRTY-ONE

The Twin Towers
Saturday Afternoon

Joker Red hugged his second in command as he, Honey B and Apolina walked into The War Room. Joker kissed Honey B on the cheek, and he looked at Apolina strangely, trying to place her.

"Aren't you cute, Joker told her and let her hand go. "What's your name?"

"Apolina Noriega," she said sweety, twirling her long braid at the end, looking like a teeny bopper. "You're the Big Boss, Joker Red. "

"You a EIE dancer?" Joker asked but then answered himself when her name popped up on the iPad Leah showed him. "Apolina Noriega. Every time I hear your last name I think of the rapper N-O-R-E-A-G-A, and the Panamanian General-"

"Manuel Antonio Noriega?" she interjected.

"Panamanian National Guard Commander; then dictator in 1945; captured during the U.S. invasion of Panama 1989 and convicted in 1992 of drug trafficking and other crimes; and I believe he did his time in Florida."

"Hm," Joker and Leah glanced of each other.

"I'm his great granddaughter," Apolina informed him.

"Aight, I'll get with you, Nori," he called her.

Ghostman and Honey B had made their way through the packed apartment socializing with a lot of familiar faces. While they did that Joker looked around until he caught Bible's eye.

"Boss," Bible said, placing a huge arm across Joker's shoulders.

"Where's my nephews?" Joker inquired.

"Calm down," Bible soothed him. "Every vehicle that arrives will be fitted with a GPS tracker. They got it covered, son."

Smoke, Rome, Brook, Jimmie 2 Tymes, Mojo, Blood Money, Streetlyfe, Big Crip, Badman, Hop, Tip Toe, Grim, Boom, Budda Clips, Rampage, Blue, Cocaine and Crime had all made the flight over from New York. They were a solid group of kids, ranging in ages, 15 to 17. They were all living that hood life, not really going anywhere except either dead or in jail. But Joker Red had plans for Young Army.

He slapped Bible on the back. "Them trackers are one

thing, but these new phones are a whole nother monster –
watch …"

He went to the front of the room.

"Aight, ATTENTION!!" Joker shouted so the meeting
could be called to order- "One by one I need everyone to
relinquish the cellphones you have and we're gonna replace
them with a really fancy encrypted phone."

"I spent a thousand on my iPhone," Carla DeLeon said,
holding it up so he could see- "I hope the new one-"

"These are three thousand minimum each," Joker cut her
short. "These are *Executive Edition* phones custom made by
iPhone and *Galaxy*. You might see the President with one like
this. Satellite capability… but your run-of-the-mill AT&T and
Verizon aren't in the picture. How much you pay a month for
your service, Carla?"

"Two hundred or so I think," the Italian dancer replied.

"No one gets a bill for these," he held up three of them.
One white, one pink, one black. "They come from my dark
web contact. The pirated services of these are from Globalstar,
ICO, Inmarsat, Motient and ORBCOMM but we won't ever
get a bill."

"I never heard of them companies," Jessika Cicero said.
"But I'll take 'free' any day."

"They provide voice and data services to thousands of
ships, planes, cars, trains, and people in parts of the world
that aren't served by cellular or traditional wired phone
networks," he explained.

Leah assisted him as she collected each person's old cellphone. "Those systems he mentioned often use constellations

of satellites in either GEO or low earth orbit to serve laptop and handset-sized mobile terminals. Such systems allow pipeline workers, merchant ships, and other mobile users to communicate even in the most remote places on "Earth."

The girls walked up and retrieved their phones one at a time. Destinee, Carla Deleon, Jessika Cicero, Isabella Caronna, Yolie Santana, Crystal, Pollyanna, Avi, Mika, Olivia, Lady, Kitten, Sinnamon, Yadi Molina, Tiera, Sherri, Jayda, Tiffani, Journee, Honey B, and Apolina.

"Ghostman?" Leah held up a black phone and he took it after relinquishing his old one. "Okay, people. Lemme show y'all, how to use them. They come with a lot of tricks."

"You gotta show me, ten times," Ghostman told her, shaking his head. "This a fly ass phone," he begrudgingly admitted.

"We gonna start usin' cryptocurrency, too." Leah revealed. "So, instead of moving big amounts of cash well just use the codes to send, receive, cash, deposit money."

Joker looked around the room and exited. He liked how a plan came together. Unbeknownst to the EIE employees coming in to get the new phones, they were not aware that they came from an underground NSA contractor who made a living on the dark web selling encrypted devices. With this particular batch he was asked to create encrypted cellphones, but to also create the "code" to allow Joker and Leah to retrieve all data from the phone's memory or history. This would include texts, voicemails, internet searches, and all audible voice texts and calls were being recorded without the user's knowledge.

The old phones collected would be scrubbed for any and all useful information by the same NSA contractor. Meanwhile Joker texted Bible.

Minutes later, Bible appeared at Joker's Penthouse where Uzenna and all of the sister-wives had the place upside down as they packed and prepared for Florida. Joker Red stopped to observe them.

"Y'all takin' two jets," he said. "I'm sending hittaz witchu, and all the shit y'all packin' need two sets."

"Why can't we use EIE'S jets?" Brittani inquired.

"Somethin' ese is goin' on," Joker told them. "But look, all y'all now have JetASAP.com app right?"

Uzenna, Coral, Asley, Leah, Eden, Valerie, Iani, Brittani and Tithi all nodded.

"Leah, sorry baby but I need you here," Joker told her. "You, too, Uzenna."

Tithi didn't like that, but she seethed in silence.

"C'mon, Bible."

They went to the back; while Tithi conjured up a plan that would keep her in Chicago for the time being. Her job required her to stay due to a personnel shortage issue at the hospital. That's what she'd tell Joker Red...

The Twin Towers
Saturday 3:00 PM

CHAPTER THIRTY-TWO

The Twin Towers
Saturday 3:00 PM

"We got all the comrades comin' in tonight," Joker revealed to him. "Maybe even earlier ...."

"Joker troubled," Bible stated.

Joker nodded. "That's true but I won't be soon when I find out who bombed us... Okay, look. I'm gonna need you to escort my cousins and nephews out to the airbase where they will work and train. Ain't nothin' I wanna keep 'em here in Chicago for and I don't want 'em getting too comfortable."

"Want me to leave with them ... now?"

"Zero-four hundred hours," Joker ordered. "Brief them

on that so they know. And for the rest of the day, keep an eye on them making sure they tag each vehicle that comes through."

Bible exited after that, and Joker put a call through to Nina.

"J.R.," She answered.

"What's happenin wit it?" He wanted to know.

"The Lieutenant has an army of security installation techs in every city in the '*Alley*' as we speak," she reported. "It makes sense. This will expedite everything."

"What if we legitimize each club?" he proposed.

"That means moving most of these locations you have in from the darkness and into the light," she said. "Once we get through the wall of Politricks that goes into these things… I believe it's smarter to be a legit businessman. My superiors would love it."

"Nail down that Central Intelligence Network location yet?" he asked.

"Anyone can lease the location," she reminded him.

"It can be anywhere, right?" He was thinking Florida.

She agreed. "Yup. But hurry up because we'll be done in a week."

They disconnected the call.

THE TWIN TOWERS

"Noriega," Joker was standing in the hallway when Apolina came straggling out of the War Room.

She looked up the hall to her left. "You scared me!" She gushed with a cute smile.

"C'mere," he called her over.

She brushed her hands down over the gray pleated skirt she wore and came to him. He was in the doorway of Romie's old apartment. They went inside and Apolina was suddenly nervous."

"Where you goin'?" he asked her.

"They all headin' out to a club and I'm goin' with the girls," she told him. "I haven't seen a couple chicks I'm cool with in a while, so we decided to meet up at *Surreal Nightlife.*"

"Will Ghost and Honey B miss you if you decide to change your mind?"

Apolina shrugged her shoulders. "I mean… you know them. They lookin' for new girls all the time."

Joker Red sat down after pouring them both a shot of Hennessy. She sat across from him and crossed her legs. "You mean… for sex, "he said.

She nodded. "Exactly."

He scratched his goatee. "Turns out you are the great granddaughter of General Noriega. Why ain't you been working in the spot you was assigned to?"

She hesitated.

"You know who I am?"

"You're "Joker Red, "she told him. "The boss."

He nodded. "Answer," he commanded.

"I'm their live-in sex toy," Apolina admitted.

Joker sat back. "Text your girls and tell them you caught a

ride home with another girl because you weren't feelin' well."

She pulled out the new encrypted cellphone and did as she was ordered. "Am I in trouble?" she inquired meekly.

"No." He sent out a text of his own.

Minutes later Bible entered the room with Leah. Apolina's heart skipped when she saw the large gleaming machete that Bible carried. Leah sat next to Apolina and handed her a yellow manila envelope.

"Open." Joker pointed at it.

Watching Bible with one eye she opened the envelope with trembling fingers.

"Go into the kitchen with that thing, Bible," Joker chuckled. "You're scarin' the pretty young mamita."

Bible disappeared.

"Leah, calm her down," Joker said.

Leah smiled and slowly kissed Apolina on her full lips. "If he says you're good, you're good."

"You're good, baby." Joker finished his drink.

Apolina nodded and opened the envelope. She saw the social media pictures of her little brother who was hospitalized with melanoma, and she instantly burst into tears.

"That's twenty thousand dollars you'll be wiring to your family," Joker said. "Okay. Lee."

Leah left them.

Apolina calmed down, drying her eyes.

"Have they helped pay his bills?" Joker asked her. "Honey and Ghost?"

She shook her head no. "A few hundred here, nice clothes,

use of nice cars, I live bill-free. Any chance I get I send money home. Honey says she loves me but it's all sex."

"Everyday? No work?"

"They don't let me work. They both just want sex with me, she revealed. "And there's a woman, a powerful woman, who even offers to buy me for twenty-five grand! I'm scared of her."

"A powerful woman," Joker repeated. *"Buy you."*

"Valoria something," she said, trying to recall her last name. "They don't let me stay in the room when she comes. There's also powerful men that they meet with, but I don't know their names. They come with bodyguards and machine guns."

"Who were they?" Joker wanted to know.

He could see her struggling to try to remember something.

"Cartels I heard," she recounted small bits and pieces of what she'd picked up. "Four men from the cartel – the *Gulf cartel.* And there's very, very, serious looking women from another cartel."

"Women?" Joker muttered. He thought quickly. "I need you to work for me. Pictures of license plates, people, download everything in their computer files to your phone and send to me. Text we each day what you see and hear."

Now she was nervous all over again.

"Nah, shorty, boss up," Joker told her, pulling out a large wad of cash. *"This* is what it's all about – not no fuckin' fear. You got a baby bro struggling wit a fuckin' skin cancer in the hospital! Bills pilin' up. And cover my back and I got yours. I don't

Want your pussy! I want you to help save my life if people are plottin on it. You do that and *Joker Red* gotchu. Aint no more like me. So whatchu say?"

She took a deep breath. "I want *all* his bills paid," she demanded.

Joker nodded. "Get me what-"

"*Upfront.* Now." She said it with her head up, sternly.

Joker smiled that signature smile of his. "Aight, I did say boss up."

"This could get me killed," she pointed out. "That bitch Honey B is a savage and I heard about Ghostman, too. He's a maniac. He kills girls and has sex with them after."

Joker had caught wind of this before, but it had sounded too incredible to believe.

"Aight ..." he paused wondering if he was putting this young woman's life at too high of a risk. "Let's get you out of here ASAP. Send me or have your family send me that boy's bills and it's done."

"They're still gonna suspect somethin' because I dipped off," she said, her mind spinning. "God why me?" she asked out of frustration.

Joker sent out a text. *"Leah, send Brittani over to Romie's with car keys. I need her to take Apolina to the hospital,"* he said as he wrote. That put a grin an Apolina's face.

Joker smiled with her. "It's nothin' like a doctor's note to throw 'em off, huh?"

Brittani arrived with her own car keys. "I'm here, Daddy. What's wrong with Apolina?"

"Food poisoning," Joker said. "C'mere, Nori."

Apolina followed him to the back of the apartment. "Look," he said, "You have gritty and grimey blood in you from your great granddad. And I'd be honored to have a bitch like you in my presence. You can do this shit. Gimme your CashApp."

She gave it to him.

He used his phone and moved some money to her CashApp.

"Ten thousand dollars?!" She cried.

"That's for taking the risk," he said. "And I love and respect Manuel Noriega. So, I gotchu shorty. Go!"

She nodded and hugged Joker, kissing his left check. "To the hospital, complain of stomach ache, food poisoning. You were eating snow crab legs with freezer burn on them," he instructed her. "I want you to call me every day," He hugged her back, and kissed her sweet pink lips causing attraction to swell between them.

After she exited, he sat down and was joined by Bible who handed him the machete. "Bible think maybe you on to something," he said.

And just like that Bible was out the door.

"Ghostman Dinero," Joker growled as he saw his own reflection in the machete's blade.

"Daddy!" Leah's voice carried from the front of the apartment. "C'mon, man!"

"What?" he called back.

"All EIE pulled up," she said.

He went to distribute the encrypted phones to his own army. *You know what?* He thought. *I was feelin' guilty at first for givin out these "encrypted" phones. But with all this suspicion of betrayal and treachery from my top man… I feel justified now.*

CHAPTER THIRTY-THREE

Ghostman's Mansion
Sunday Afternoon

Ghostman had, indeed, went out with the EIE dancers the previous night and he didn't come home until almost 1:00 PM. When he did Honey B was at the front door clearly upset. She grabbed him by the hand and pulled him into the empty library office.

"What're you trippin' about?" he asked his wife as he snatched his hand away.

"*You* was with the Italian gid, Jessika Cicero!"

"So what?" he shot back. "You left with Kitten and Mika.
"

"We all came back here," she said in a hush. "Her girls,

Carla Deleon and Isabella Caronna are, calling Police, Fire, hospitals, *Joker Red*. She's missing!"

"After I was with her, she bounced," he told her. He tried to leave but she stood in his way. "Can I shower and take a shit? I'm tired."

"Joker called looking for Jessika," Honey informed Ghostman." You gotta call him.

Ghostman pulled her away from the door and left her standing there. He went upstairs to kiss their sleeping baby first. Then he went to use the toilet. While he was in the shower Honey B came into the bathroom.

"What did you do with her?" She asked him calmly.

"I told you, she left-"

"¡Mentiroso!" she spat. "Don't lose my respect… No lies!"

He turned the shower off. "The only one tellin' lies around here is you."

"Don't turn this shit on me," she stated with controlled anger because Kitten and Mika were in the room asleep.

"We was *been* supposed to be takin over this entire operation," he reminded her. "Months are goin' by, you had the baby and-"

"What are you talking about?" she interrupted. "We're making money on our own that he was never going to cut you in on. As his number two you should get fifty percent. You hardly got *ten*. We're making ten, fifteen, percent of his net because of *my* plan. How else would we afford that Bugatti you dropped two million on?"

"Bitch I had millions stashed I coulda used for that shit," he shot back.

"*Exactly*, and you still got it," she said, crossing her aims." I'm doin *exactly* as planned. Everywhere Red has set up shop we now have a tattoo shop. In those shops are Albanian tattoo artists, beautiful, young, fresh faced sex girls with fine tatted bodies, scanty clothing, cleaning the shops; cashiers… irresistible, well-trained. They find out from drug dealers, going members, what they need, and we'll supply it. Coke, dope, meth, weapons, encrypted cell-phones, and of course the gift that keeps on giving: Sex with our fine young girls. *Where have I lied?*" She demanded to know.

Ghostman dried off and applied a Muslim oil and lotion combo to his skin. "I been controllin' the demons… but last night I lost it and…" he trailed off with a nonchalant shrug.

"And what?" she pushed.

"Somethin' about her," he said with a shrug. "She was lookin' good. Ass was fatter. She had her seat back literally fingering her pussy as we drove towards the Towers. She had the TV on Pornhub and kept fuckin wit me. That raw female pussy heat…she fucked wit me."

"How? Fucked witchu, how?"

"Rubbin' her wet fingers on my lips and nose," he said. "I lost it."

"So you killed her for that?" Honey said more than asked.

"No…" He turned to his wife, his penis so hard and swollen that it stood out like a diving board.

She looked at it. "So why? Why'd you kill her?"

"I pulled over on a side street and… she wanted head," he admitted, "Said something about her man would know if she fucked. So I ate her but… I lost it. I beat her… Fucked her. Choked her until I knew she was dead. And then I finished."

"While she was dead," Honey whispered as she took ahold of his penis and stroked him. "While she was limp?"

Honey squirted lotion on her hands and made him sit on the toilet. She looked up at him and jacked his long, thick, and meaty dick. He sat back and relaxed.

"You like killing huh, Papi?"

He nodded, his dick feeling so good.

"Why?" She was trying to understand.

"Because they're so warm still," he replied pumping his hips up and down. "So quiet … and pretty."

Just before he was about to orgasm the bathroom door opened and in came Kitten.

"Ohh, shit, you guys!" She giggled. "I have to pee so bad!!"

"Dann!" Ghostman muttered.

Kitten was about 5 feet 7 inches, black hair, slim and cute. When she smiled, she flashed what looked like baby teeth because her teeth were kind of small for a 22 year old woman.

Ghostman wiped the only lotion off of his privates and Honey B cleaned up her hands. They gave the bathroom to Kitten and went into the bedroom. However, Mika was sprawled access the sheets naked except for a pink thong.

"Damn, y'all had it poppin' in here last night, huh?" Ghostman said, looking all up between the light-skinned Black girl's freckled asscheeks. She must have had a bushy pussy because he saw wisps of hair flowing out of the sides of the thin band of cloth covering her pussy.

. . .

Honey B shucked her robe and climbed next to Mika on all fours with her asscheeks bussed open. "C'mon, Papi. You got me hot. Fuck me."

He gave her exactly what she asked for. Mika and Kitten were drawn into the early afternoon fun.

Later, after Mika and Kitten exited in their own vehicles, Honey B and Ghostman still had to deal with the matter of Jessika.

"Anybody check on Apple?" he asked her. "I heard she was sick last night."

"Yeah," Honey B replied. "Somethin' she ate at the Towers gave her mild food poisoning. They treated her and she's in her room."

Ghostman went to check in on her. She was lying back on her bed with one hand on her new phone and the other inside of a bowl of fresh green seedless grapes while Ghostman's newborn son lay awake at her side.

"You feelin' better?" He asked Apolina.

"Mm hm," she nodded. "Tryna learn more about this phone. This is one fancy piece of machinery."

"You like it?" He asked sitting next to her.

She nodded yes. "There's a million movies, millions of songs, they've pirated *everything*."

I can even go to *OnlyFans* and watch anyone for free! They got all the dark web functions; the onion router is all set up. This must be the most illegal phone on the planet! Can you imagine pedophile havin' this shit?

"Why?" he asked as she displayed a few things to him.

"International child porn, live child porn, *auctions...*" she rattled off a few. "No GPS. It shifts from satellite to satellite, and so many routers, the FBI prolly gets lost tryna track a pedophile in this infinite cyberspace. This is exactly the type of technology Russian and North Korean hackers hide behind."

"No GPS trackin'?" he asked, thinking about where he'd dispose of Jessika's body.

Apolina shook her head. "Nope. Unless you were on an Amerikkan satellite for an extended period which this type of encrypted phone won't allow. It shifts satellites every couple of minutes, And all calls, text, voicemails, emails are lost. There's no historic retrieval capability. I tried."

That made Ghostman trust the new phones.

"Papi can I have one of these?" she asked him sweetly.

"What, another phone?"

She shook her head no, pointing at his son.

"You want a baby??" he asked her.

"Stephen Adams, the 2nd," she said.

He looked at his son, Stephen Adams, Jr., and back at her. "It has to be an accident-quote unquote-ya dig? Cuz she ain't having that. Youse her girl, and you feelin' me like that?"

She nodded. "You can't be sexing me like that and I don't catch feelings for both of y'all. And you nuttin' all up in me... I can't help lovin' you."

"I'll talk to her then." She was making his dick hard.

Apolina shook her head frantically like. "No! We'll do what you said. But can me and you do it more?"

He kissed her tenderly. "Yeah."

"I mean without her in the room?"

"Sshh!" he nodded not wanting Honey B to hear. "Yeah I got you, mami."

About an hour later the baby was asleep and Apolina was in the bathroom after showering and touching up her toenails with a peach-colored polish. Ghostman entered her room wearing only a pair of black sweatpants. He locked the door and found Apolina inside of the bathroom. He went right up to her, bent down and kissed her.

"Mm, what was that for?" she asked him. She pushed him away as well. "No—where's Honey at?"

"She went out," he told her. "When you was talking earlier…you made me hard as hell. C'mon gimme dat lil Panamanian pussy. Imma fuck you, buss a nut all over the egg wit this big dick and black juicy balls. You hear me?"

Ghostman made it hard for her to say no with the hot way he was talking to her. He watched her put both arms high above her head and he pulled her nightgown off leaving her wearing matching pink and white lacy panties and a bra. He pushed down his sweatpants and kicked them off.

"I see how Little Ghost looks at you and Honey B…and how you look at them and I swear to god, Papi, I have your babies. Just protect me and love me like I love you," she was saying as they lay side by side in her bed and he started in on her pretty breasts and succulent nipples.

"Shit you love me, mami?" he asked kissing, tonguing, sucking and licking her breasts. She moaned and let him turn her onto her belly.

"I do...I do..."

He kissed her sweet tattooed buttocks and inhaled her steaminess. She was still moist from the bath. He opened her holes and she smelled like the jasmine soap and soft-scented body wash. She didn't even smell like her own body yet. But she was juicier than water where her vagina opened. He was up on her and inside of her and loud gasp let him know that she was all the way with it.

Slowly he humped in and out of her from behind while talking nasty in her right ear, sucking on it, biting her neck, squeezing her titties from underneath. She could tell that she'd gotten into his brain because his dick was so hard and his balls so fat and close to exploding with millions of sperm. He *slap! slap! slap! slam! slam! slam! deep and deeper* and she rode backwards making him feel that young pussy loving him and causing him to want to shove his face in both their hot juices. And that's exactly what he did, too.

"Gimme this sweet ass, mami!" he said as kissed her anus and ten her swollen cunt lips. "Turn over."

They were both bathed in sweat when she let him re-enter her wet pink pussy missionary. One thing about Ghostman he could fuck like a well-trained porn superstar. Apolina had one of those small clean-shaven pussies that could orgasm like crazy and then she'd shut down – out of juice. Honey B could cum for hours, even while only sucking a dick.

"Oooooooouuuuuuu!!! You makin' me cum! You makin' me cum! You makin' me cum! You makin' aaaaannnnnnggghh! Fuck! She screamed as she fucked him hard."

"Here it-it's cummin', Apple!!" he whimpered. He *slap!*

slap! slapped! Hard and skeeted his hot nut all the way up inside her belly. He whispered as he fucked her slow for a minute. "You want that baby I gotchu mami. Every chance we get Imma buss all up in you."

She ran her hands all over his soaking wet body. "That was so good. So sinful."

"Damn you got a small pussy!"

"Your dick is fuckin'…how they say it? A *whopper!*" she said and laughed.

He smiled. "Give ya *chocha* back to that twelve-year-old you stole it from!"

She kissed him. "I love you like I love your son."

They kissed real genuine kisses. He saw her for an ally now and got that much closer to her. He got up but she pulled him back down to her.

"Where you going?" she feigned a kittenish whine.

"To shower. You want me to smell like your pussy cream?"

"Yeah," she said. But then quickly changed her mind. "No."

Ghostman chuckled and left her laying there not knowing that she was conning him.

CHAPTER THIRTY-FOUR

Joker Red's Penthouse
Tuesday Evening

Joker Red listened to Uzenna and Tithi saying mean and snide comments to each other in the kitchen the day after the other sister-wives, and several EIE hittaz, had travelled to Fort Lauderdale to lock down the perfect land deal for their family.

All of the children had gone with Coral, Ashley, Eden, Valerie, Iani, Brittani, La Colombiana, Ceasar, Bible, and Breach. Only Baby Joker remined and he was currently with Amelia and Goliath who were out shopping. Amelia was Baby Joker's Mexican nanny, the one Uzenna had hit in the head before taking Baby Joker.

Leah was seated at the kitchen table eating a turkey sandwich. "Both of you guys need to stop this back and forth before one of you goes too far," Leah chided them.

"I don't see what he even sees in her," Uzenna said, rolling her eyes. "A pregnant cat is cuter than she is."

Joker appeared at the mouth of the kitchen completely naked, soaking wet, fresh off of a grueling one-hour workout on the Peloton, followed by a shower and a hot soak in the Jacuzzi. He had heard enough between the two women and the time had come to confront the elephant in the room.

"You been back what-? A week?" Joker nearly was growling at Uzenna.

She stood there frozen.

"Why you disrespecting your sister-wife?" Joker demanded an answer.

"This the most you've said to me," Uzenna held her hands on the countertop as she spoke. "And that bitch ain't no sister-wife of mine."

"You called me a fucking *coward*! You ridiculed me in front of everybody!" he hissed. "And then you...*took...my...son! My firstborn child, whose birthright is everything I own!*"

Leah's mouth was open. Tithi was shaking. Joker was so emotional that his heart had opened and broken all over his face.

"Didn't I say I'ma take you out of slavery?!" he asked passionately. "Answer me!"

Uzenna nodded, feeling crushed. "Yes!"

"I put that together! And since that night have you had to

whore yourself, suck on them nasty white cocks, or stand by why any of your sisters had to still go through that?!"

"No!" Uzenna cried. "No!" she cried louder, shaking her head.

"Have you had to whore, Leah?!" he boomed.

Leah shook her head.

"I made you a *boss* didn't I?"

Uzenna nodded. "Yes, Joker, you did! And. I'm sorry! I'M SORRY! I fucked up! But you're *crucifying me*! You won't talk to me! You won't *touch* me! You *replaced* me!"

"No," he said. "*You* did the harm. *You*. Not me. You need to humble yourself and understand that this family is an empire and a privilege. You can't disrespect nobody. Especially when you fucked up. You just said so!"

Uzenna nodded. "Humble myself how? I wanna do it. Show me."

"All of y'all c'mere:" he ordered. "This will be painful, Uzenna, but redemption costs."

He sat down on a long backed cushioned chair in the master bedroom and ordered Uzenna to undress, She wiped her remaining tears and did as he'd demanded.

"Y'all undress too, and sit on the bed," he said to Leah and Tithi.

"Tithi's pregnant...it's time Uzenna and Leah to get pregnant again, too."

Leah got undressed and felt the moist warmth of excitement spread down between her legs and up through her breasts. Tithi squirmed with a strange sense of sexual delight because she had no idea what he was going to do.

"Over here," he told Uzenna. "Over my lap so that ass is right here. Feet on the flood…that's right."

She was doing as he'd instructed. "Leah, c'mere," he ordered. "Hold your hand, close your fingers, and spank her."

Leah was so girly that she brought her small hand down more like a pat on the back. Joker chuckled.

"Doctor Patel," he said as he felt Uzenna's ass grind up and down. "You deliver a baby yet?"

"I'm not in Pediatrics. I'm in trauma," she said, Shaking her head. She tied her long black hair in an up-do ponytail real quick. "But I can spank her," she assured him. She privately thought, *what a beautiful ass.*

Joker smiled. "That's good. Spank her for bein' mean. Leah go get a belt and several long silk scarves. A leather belt."

Uzenna was no longer nervous. Her pussy was actually on fire, but she didn't let on how turned on she was: "What are y'all gonna do to me?" She asked in a nervous voice. "Please don't hurt me? Please?"

Joker brought his hand down hard on her tattooed, honey-hued, booty cheeks. "Who gave you permission to speak?" he scolded her. "You've been a bad girl and bad girls become slaves and sex toys. You hear me?"

He spanked her hard on the opposite cheek, causing her to wince painfully.

"Oww! Yes, Daddy! Yes!" she squealed and reached back with her left hand to rub the sting off.

"Don't touch!" he demanded, smacking her hands away.

"This is how y'all do it…" he said to Leah and Tithi. "This is how you control a sweet little bitch like her when her head gets too big. Tie up her hands and I mean tight."

Leah and Tithi worked together to tie up her wrists. "Unnhh," Uzenna whined and writhed in a circle. "Lemme suck your monster banana, baby, and tongue your asshole… or lemme eat Tithi's cunt. Her pregnant little Indian cunt. I'll do anything to humble myself before this family!"

"Yes!" he spanked her left cheek and then her right. He spoke nasty words to her. "Now y'all. *Hard.*"

Tithi took all of her hurt and frustration out on Uzenna for talking bad to her. She slapped those beautiful buttocks.

"Harder!" he shouted.

Whap! Tithi went on the left cheek.

Slap! Leah spanked her harder.

Uzenna was actually squirming in pain now because Joker wasn't playing. Her pussy lips were glistening with evidence of her heat.

"That thing red now!" He noticed the red swelling welts all over her ass. He also felt the shiny sheen of perspiration that had broken out all over her body. "Open them legs… *wider!*"

"My shoulder and legs feel like rubber," she whined. Holding herself across his lap meant having her bound hands on the floor and herself across his lap meant having her bound hands on the floor and her feet there as well. But that sweet banging ass was bussed open.

He dismissed how she felt. He could smell the scent of her arousal. "Despite being punished for your sins…you've been waggin' your ass and tryna grind your throbbin clit into me…all your wet slutty juices have been seeping down onto me. Is that right? Am I lying? This feels good to you, doesn't it? You love the pain!"

He found her clitoris and she gasped from the jolt of pleasure she was now feeling. A salty sweet honey trickled from her pussy.

"Leah, lube your hand up," he told her as he got up and led Uzenna to the bed. He used scarves to tie her arms forward to the bed posts. He tied one leg to the bed's end post and had Leah insert her fingers slowly in and out of Uzenna's wet opening. "You're gonna *fist* that pussy Leah, and I mean I want you to fuck her *hard*. Be merciless."

Uzenna was face down, biting and howling her pleasure into the blankets. Leah was experienced with *lesbian fisting* and had done it with Uzenna before. While she did that, Joker made sure Tithi held Uzenna's free leg secure. Joker took the belt he had and brought it down hard over Uzenna's ass, careful not to hit Leah.

"Oh, god!" she gasped at the stinging *whap!* of the leather belt.

Leah had her entire hand inside of her sister-wife now and she slowly made a fist. As soon as she did Uzenna felt it and her ass started doing slow juicy twirls around and around Leah's little fist. Her pussy hole clamped tightly around her small wrist. She sobbed from the pleasure, wanting more.

"Daddy I'm fuckin' her!" Leah decreed, feeling her own vagina leaking cream.

"I wanna see you poundin' and punchin' them slutty

walls of hers!" he commanded as he whipped her golden red buttocks again and again. Pinch her clit with the other hand… Tithi get there, and I want her face in your face pussy while you get at her breasts. Squeeze them nipples hard! Suck that Indian cunt, Zen!

Tithi did as he said. The room smelled like Uzenna's high quality pussy. Her squirty vaginal juices were soaking up everything. Her scent drove not only him crazy, but the girls were thoroughly turned on as well. As soon as that little Indian pussy was in front of her face, Uzenna inhaled that fresh pregnant little thing and went to licking, nibbling and snacking.

The belt whistled down upon Uzenna's ass at first and then he started lashing her back as well. The pain was great but the pleasure she felt was even better.

"Harder, Leah!" he urged her on. "Fuck this bad girl… Fuck her harder! Harder, Leah!"

He was staring at the fisting and god, what a turn on! Whap! He kept up the whipping. Tithi held Uzenna's head and gyrated her pussy in a tight circle going clockwise, getting all of that Indian girl dew up in her face!

Whap! Back to the ass. Whap! Whap! Whap! Whap! He was maniac with the whipping and Uzenna hollered tears of joy and pain she never knew. When he'd seen that her skin had finally opened, he felt she'd had enough.

He united her and she continued to make love to Tithi with her mouth. "Mm, you still love me, Tithi?" Uzenna asked her. "I love you. I love this pussy!"

"Oh, yes, I love you, Zenna," Tithi nodded.

Joker maneuvered his wife onto her left side while Leah continued the delicious, sticky-sounding fist fucking. He spooned her from the rear and opened her sore right asscheek and guided his golden-brown cucumber right up to her tiny anal orifice.

"I'm gonna finally fuck your ass, mommy," he whispered harshly to her. "Open it up…loosen that thing up and let your daddy in there, okay?"

She nodded. "Fuck my ass, Daddy. I've been a bad girl. Take my ass."

He slowly penetrated, using the Astro glide lubricant Leah provided. He pushed two inches in and mini-fucked her for a few minutes just like that. The head popped into her and it felt wet, slippery and delicious.

"Keep fisting me!" She whimpered through clenched teeth. "Ohhhh, Leeeaaahhhh, fuck!! D-d-aaaaddddyyyy! Fuck my ass more now! Oooouuuuuueeee! How much is that?!"

"'Bout five, mami," he huffed as he sawed it in and out of her tight musky depths, "'Bout half. Oh shit, your ass feel good wrapped around me, baby."

He sent all of it plunging deep inside of her fine back end and she yelped with glee, and pain as he squeezed her sore buttocks. At the same time he plugged her sensually, with his big ten-inch member, Leah focused on fisting and sucking her clit for mind blowing pleasure.

Uzenna's body froze all of a sudden and she let out a howling scream as her damn broke and squirted her clearish colored cream all over Leah's face and fingers.

"Leah!" Joker grabbed the petite Leah and kissed her after

pulling out of Uzenna. He laid Leah back and fucked her hard and passionately.

"Ooooouu, Daddy," Leah gasped opening her small white legs wider for him.

He looked down at it her sweet face and she put the hand she'd been fisting *Uzenna* with under his nose and he went at the scent he caught. She wiped it all over his cheeks and face and he bit her neck like a vampire as he fucked her harder and harder.

"Oooohhh my fuckin' god!" Leah cried as she whipped her hips around and around his huge dick. "I'm cumming!"

Uzenna grabbed his balls from behind and softly caressed them. That caused him to explode.

"I'm cuuummmiiinnn' mommie!" He cried and kissed Leah. "Oooouuu, shit, baby!"

Uzenna was shaking and crying. The emotion, the hot sex, the adrenaline clutched her breasts and private parts or something. "I love you and I'm sorry. I was so stupid. Joker you and you sisters of mine I'm so very lucky."

As she spoke her fingers were dipping in and out of her pussy and the still wide-open anal cavity which was swollen and red. Just as swollen and red as her sore cunt lips. Uzenna got between Leah's legs and laid on her stomach. She wanted to lick up all of Joker's semen.

"OOOHHHH shit!" Leah gasped. Uzenna lick her pink twat clean while holding onto those thick hips of hers. Leah was a lovely sized white chick who was Joker's obvious favorite among the white girls. Her body was amazing.

Leah had one of those Instagram model bodies and her

face? — Just incredible. Anyone following IG models such as *NIXLYNKASAYASHI*, AKA *Nixlynka the 13th* could easily imagine the body comparison. Guve Nixlynka the blond hair sparkling eyes-100% match. When Uzenna was done licking up every drop of Joker's cum Uzenna seized Joker's half-hard dick and she nursed it back to life. She sucked that mighty, mighty beast down into her throat…looking lovingly and dazzingly at the love of her life and father of her universe…

She communicated her submissiveness and her desire for forgiveness with her amazingly beautiful eyes. She would bob her head up and down, letting him fuck her face with his monster cock. He held her and pushed the entire length into her throat until his big warm balls covered her whole chin. He'd then-maybe-take out two inches and keep fucking in and out of her throat. She looked so sweet.

"GODDDDAAAAMMMM you can swallow that big dick!!" he shouted, falling back against the pillows. She had a grip on his long pipe, spitting on it and stroking it. She pushed his legs up…ass-licked him, twirling and toilet-bowling his rim. "Bitch Imma fuck you up if you-" But he let her mouth have his butthole.

Like most men he tried to front like he didn't love it when his wives "rim-jobbed" him but that shit drove him nuts. *He was gangster through and through; tried, tested, never failed* but his women were heartless savage, vampires who did what they wanted and *needed*. That's what they called it. For example, Uzenna had told him that she had a powerful urge to suck his cock, balls and she couldn't explain why but eating his asshole was something she was *drawn* to.

"No different from you doin' it to me, Daddy," she'd said a long while back. *"The same way you lose it for the musky scent of pussy and eating and tonguing our asses...let us have our needs satisfied too. Why men be so weird? Youse a sexy light skinned fly nigga wit a dozen bad bitches you own. Me and you are married! Man and woman. A man is a homo when he wit a man. But what a man and woman do in bed is heterosexual. It's-"*

He'd cut her off back then by kissing her big juicy lips and entering her. Right now Uzenna was killing him by slowly jacking that beast while her mouth stayed busy. Teasingly sucking, kissing and licking his hairless perineum and butt crack.

"Imma kill yo ass," he said in a whisper as she sucked his balls, gave them the most gentle perfect squeezes. Her middle finger diddled in a circle around the edges of his anus. His cock inflated to the hardest and largest he'd ever been and the precum was coming out of him like a small stream. She fisted his long, beautiful monster, licking the huge vein underneath it prior to reburying it in her mouth. She took no time to let it slide on in past her tonsils. One hand on the dripping wet trunk and the other on his balls she picked up the up and down, up, down, up, down, up, down pace. With her saliva, his salty sweet precum against his smooth golden skin inside of her slippery mouth she had him feeling like he was inside a warm wet tight virgin cunt.

"You still wanna kill me?" she asked as she took a second to pop that behemoth sized cock out. But right back in it went.

"Fuck no. Hell no. I'll give you any fuckin' thing. Just

don't stop!" he gasped as he humped his hot wet dick back into, her throat. "Lemme cum. Stop squeezin' my shit-stoppin' da cum from bussin' out!"

"Ok…I gotchu," she whispered and spit mad saliva into her right hand. She had him feenin' for that super duper sloppy head. He didn't care that she was eating his asshole and stroking that monster meat and balls with both hands. "Fuck my face, Daddy. Fuck my mouth-hard. Cum inside it."

Uzenna performed like a champ for the other girls. She handled his penis like Tiffany Haddish handled that banana and grapefruit in the movie *Girls Trip*. Only Uzenna had no bananas or grapefruit. She would press her middle finger beneath his balls whenever he was ready to nut. She knew that since he was so turnt up that his cum would blast everywhere.

He was fucking her face harder…then clutching the back of her head for more leverage…fucking deep into her throat-her esophagus. He was moaning and then…she had buried her middle finger inside of him and he froze.

"Bitch, what--?" he started.

But then, she was back to sucking him while stroking his prostate. The instant shock and pleasure made him scream in a deep low howl.

"Glrrrp, slrrrp, mmmphuh! Annngh!" She cried while stealing a gulp of air through her mouth. She'd ingested so much semen that she nearly choked on it. And when she coughed while his massive glans was still caught down her throat she had coughed up a glob of off-white sperm through the nostrils.

Leah and Tithi were staring with their mouths open. Leak looked at Tithi while mouthing the synonym *"O-M-F-G!"* Tithi, in turn, nodded stating, *"shit!"*as she continued to watch Uzenna remove her finger which caused Joker to release even more cum which Uzenna was managing to capture, lick up and swallow all that she could find. Moments later, both Joker and Uzenna, awash in fresh perspiration, collapsed on the bed next to each other.

"Fuck!" Joker shouted looking at his hands shake. He stared at Uzenna, but she was quiet, her lips swollen, cum glistening on her chin and neck.

"What about the finger, Daddy?" Leah asked.

He just shook his head. "I just wanna know if everybody good. Is Uzenna forgiven for her sins?"

The girls answered yes.

"That's it then," Joker declared "I love y'all."

"We love you, too, Daddy," Tithi said with a bright smile. She leaned down and kissed Uzenna.

The hatchet was buried.

CHAPTER THIRTY-FIVE

Joker's Penthouse
Wednesday Morning

"Ow! Ow! Ow!" Uzenna moaned in pain as Tithi applied a fast-healing ointment to Uzenna's back and buttocks as she lay on the sun deck on her stomach.

Joker came out and sat across from them. The sight of him reminded her ass and her vagina of the black out delicious orgasms she derived from that twisted mind of his. The pain she felt now was making her pussy and asshole clench open and closed in memory of him. *Oh my god I can't believe I want to be whipped,* she thought.

"What?" Tithi broke the silence as Leah brought out hot

bagels, butter, beef omelets and orange juice for everybody.

"I'm in pain," Uzenna told Tithi and Leah who came near enough to hear her. "But…seein' him-and y'all-makes me so wet right now!"

"Really?" Leah asked. "You're not, like mad?"

"God no!" Uzenna shook her head. "I mean I had an orgasm in my ass *and* pussy! Now she won't dry back up!"

"I didn't get fucked," Tithi complained, feeling dejected. "But I'm with you. I had big, big orgasms from you, Uzenna. And watching that whipping…the fisting…and the anal sex was mind-blowing. Then when he was inside Leah…did you see her rubbing your juices all in his nose, face and all over?"

"Hell yeah!" Uzenna nodded. "Once he gets that pussy aroma in him it makes him lose it."

"He is such a freak," Leah whispered. "You want another baby?"

Uzenna nodded. "Yeah. I mean we can only have babies for a limited time so…Yeah. Why, you don't?"

"I do," Leah said. "But David Two came a little early and was six pounds. So…"

"Don't worry," Tithi said. "Worry is stress. Think positive and-"

"What are y'all huddlin' about?" Joker Red interrupted.

"Nothin' Girl talk," Tithi informed him.

"Like what?" he probed.

"Pregnancy health, etcetera," Tithi educated him.

He looked at the three of them and Uzenna's exposed bottom.

"There's another shipment of encrypted phones coming." Joker had a tight face as he said it.

He loved Don Braga, Vinnie and all the other Mafia associates that he did business with. He hated to have to give the encrypted phones to the mob just like he hated to have to pass them out to his own organization. Because even though the phones were encrypted, he could, through the CIA, retrieve everything off of the phone's memory.

Nina had stressed to him over and over that she was not assigned to collect information from the Mafia or EIE. However, since discovering the identities of those who'd bombed Joker Red's loved ones was in the CIA's best interests, Nina had been greenlighted on sealing Joker Red the shipment of flawed encrypted cellphones.

"There can't be one arrest connected to these phones," Joker had demanded a promise from Nina. *"Nobody usin' me for no stoolie."*

"We. Don't. Care!" She had exclaimed. "We want you to find who killed your people. And for you to know everything about what your people are thinking, saying and doing in the street and behind closed doors. Most of all the phones do indeed have GPS so you can see where they've been and where they're going."

Nina said it best to him. *"You can't be afraid of being a king, Joker. What you have with CIA/DOD is power. Use it. Keeping tabs, recordings, faking people out with bogus or flawed encryption devices is not being a rat. It's knowledge. If you're a rat, then so is every powerful man that ever lived. If you're given the chance to have power over others you damned well better know where they've been and where they're going. We already know what we want to know about Frank Braga and EIE. Now we want you to know."*

"I'll accept the phones," Leah said to him. "I thought we gave 'em all out."

"We got to provide them for the Braga's," Joker told her.

"Frank and Vinnie?" she frowned. "Or for their whole-?"

"It'll be two to three hundred more devices," he said.

"Oh my god!" Leah whined. "Who's gonna help me? Tithi's goin' to the trauma center."

Joker ignored her. "I'm headin' out. And, by the way, I was texted about two more missions we gotta do. I don't know when, but I was notified."

"What?" It was Tithi's turn to frown now. "Where?"

"I don't have any details yet," Joker said. "But you put in that resignation notice today."

He hugged and kissed the girls and exited.

CHAPTER THIRTY-SIX

The Twin Towers

He approached his prized Bugatti Chiron but changed his mind when he noticed that the protective leather and vinyl cover was secured to it with small locks and all. He paid his nanny Amelia's husband to keep all of the cars cleaned and under strict watch 24-7 so this was either his doing or the doing of one of his crew. Either way Joker didn't want to get his hands dirty screwing around with the car cover nor waste any more time on it.

He headed out to Winthrop to pop up on Ghostman about Jessika Cicero coming up missing. Those closest to her-like Carla DeLeon and Isabella Caronna-were blowing up his phone about it and Jessika's family had already contacted the police. Just because EIE had some powerful forces backing them up did not make them immune to trouble like this.

Then, there was an even more worrisome issue looming. Jessika had been getting close to Vinnie Braga lately. Joker Red was on his way to Ghostman's after choosing to drive one of his bullet-proof, bomb-proof, Cadillac SUV's when several "Photo Messages" came through on his encrypted phone. His *truly* encrypted phone.

"Apolina Noriega," he muttered as he cruised up the highway. "Let's see whatchu got, Nori."

Apolina: That Valoria woman is here," Apolina texted him. "With those cartel men and women, I told you about. I couldn't get any closer, but I did manage to put the GPS tracker on her car, a white Maserati, MC 20. Photo take of everyone.

Joker Red had a cold grimace on his face because he had been feeling like his main man—Ghostman Dinero—was doing something treacherous in the dark. And perhaps he was…and it had nothing to do with harming Joker, EIE or their associates. *Perhaps.* Joker had to find out.

Joker sent the photos to Nina with a text.

Joker: I've developed an informant on the inside of the GD mansion. She spoke of a powerful woman named Valoria, sending pic of her license plate, and several of Valoria and her cartel associates. I need identities, intel, ASAP."

Nina: Where are you?

Joker: Nearing GD mansion to recon ppl in pics.

Nina: I need you to return home, now! We know this Valoria. Waiting on facial rec for others. Fall back. Trust me.

Joker didn't understand but he turned into a gas station and sat there with his mind spinning. He shot Nina a text.

Joker: *Returning. You better have answers goddammit!*

To himself he whispered. "Somethin's up. Somethin' bad."

Prior to hitting the road back home Joker Red sent his number two man a text.

Joker: Jessika Cicero…Where the fuck is she? The heat is on top of this one and so's the Bragas because that was Vinnie's mistress.

Ghostman wrote right back to him, denying any knowledge or involvement in her disappearance but Joker knew Ghostman better than anyone. Joker Red had heard the rumors of what he likes and what he has been suspected of doing.

Cheekie was a missing woman who had never made it back to Mississippi when she'd been ejected from the team.

Esmeralda Cartagena was another young dancer that had mysteriously disappeared.

There were whispers of other girls that had met the same fate and Joker Red was feeling partially responsible because he's the one who had given Ghostman so much power in the organization to begin with. *Knowing the secrets we had both left behind in Kandahor and Chaman and Quetta, Afghanistan. The war crimes we both committed. Mine were more along the lines of murder…savage decapitations and torture and murder.* Joker recounted as he drove home. He made it to the Twin Towers and sat there, glued to his seat thinking about everything.

He texted Tithi.

Joker: Where you at?

Tithi: The hospital. W'sup bby?

Joker: Miss u,

Tithi: Awww. Love u. Be home @ 9.

Joker: Aiight. I'm pickin' u up. Will text u when I'm downstairs.

He turned off the Caddy and went upstairs.

He was trying to get the thought of Quetta (Afghanistan) out of his mind, but they were there loud like war drums in the Congo and incendiary shells whistling through the sky overhead and exploding as they hit targets "that" night. His unit had been dispatched to rescue a Black female doctor from a group of Al Qaeda soldiers.

Joker Red (Sgt. Hodges), Ghostman and fourteen other Rangers-most who were already EIE goons-had raided a house in the village and killed most of the terrorists. When the firefight was over only Joker, Ghostman, Ground War and Fast Eddie had remained while inside of the house where they'd discovered several kilograms of heroin…

The Afghanistan War

"EVERYONE ELSE BACK TO BASE WITH THE DOCTOR," JOKER TOLD his team. "Ghostman stays. So does Eddie and Grounder."

Grounder was another alias for the Ground War alias. Joker had instructed his unit to return within the hour and report to their

Staff Sergeant that Joker and the others were staying to search and then burn the place.

Bodies were everywhere. The Al Qaeda scum who owned the house had a plain-looking wife of about 37, a 7-year-old son and a 13-year-old daughter. There was also an older man. That's who Joker tortured by cutting off his right thumb. Ghostman stood there nodding his approval with a smile on his face one moment and the next moment he was gone.

Joker made the old man tell him where the real supply of Afghan heroin was being held at. The old man had fainted after his second finger was amputated. He used an electric hand-held lock cutting tool which was ran by a lithium rechargeable battery.

"The fuck up!" Joker shouted as he ruthlessly front slapped and then back slapped the older man. The man regained consciousness. "Get 'im wet. Eddie."

Fast Eddie lifted his Ruger Mini 14 assault rifle, with the 30-round clip which was packed full of .223 Black Rhino bullets.

"Nah, nah-wit water." Joker put his hand on the weapon as he gave the order.

Eddie doused the old man with a full bottle of cold water, waking him up completely. The old man held his hand up and Eddie chuckled. "Son. Da old head tryna point but he ain't got a pointer fingah! Ha! Ha! Ha! Ha! Ha!" Eddie's raucous laughter reverberated throughout the house.

Joker shoved the old man into the kitchen where he said something Arabic. Joker understood a little of language, so he pulled out the refrigerator and saw a loose plywood panel behind it. He snatched it off and threw it across the kitchen. He looked inside and there were only four more kilograms but also a small black box made *of mahogany. He opened it. A second later he was staring at the old man again and handing Ground War a flash drive.*

"Uncut diamonds," Fast Eddie said pouring them out onto the kitchen table. "No cash in there Sarge?"

"No cash," Joker answered him.

"What's their money called again? The dinar?" Ground War asked. "Joker knows all the currencies."

"The dinar is Iraq, Algeria-spots like that…Kuwait, I can't think of 'em all right now," Joker told them. "But Afghanistan has the Afghani."

Joker removed his all black "K-bar" knife, held it tight in his grip. "See what's on that file, GW."

GW (Ground War) removed his backpack his laptop computer, once it was set up and prepared, they began to watch the video content. It was a video of an Al Shebab leader speaking first in a Nguni tongue and then Arabic. In the background were Black males and Black females who were being forced to labor inside of what looked like diamond mines AKA Blood Diamonds.

"They had somethin' goin' on," Joker spoke up. "These fuckers were exchanging 'H' for blood diamonds…and Al Shebab wanted that doctor so they could have her on their team when babies are born."

Ground War and Eddie both had scowls on their faces.

"Why? Ay! Old man!" Eddie yelled at him.

Joker cooled Eddie down. "Just hold his ass still."

Ground War and Eddie held him down on the kitchen floor.

Suddenly Joker had a change of heart. "Pack up and take cover outside. When yose have eyes on the unit transport hit me on COM. Pack it up. Don't lose that loot, fast."

When they exited, Joker looked down at the moaning old timer. He took the K-Bar combat blade and then sank it straight up and in the heart of the enemy, killing him. They didn't leave anyone to tell them what had happened.

Joker heard Ghostman in the adults bedroom, so he opened the door. "C'mon. nigga! Shit. I shoulda fuckin' knew!"

Ghostman had the mother's hands tied over her head to the brass headboard. Both of the woman's ankles were tied to the wide left and wide right bed posts so that her legs were splayed open sort of like the "wishbone" on a chicken.

Ghostman was raping the 13-year-old daughter while forcing her to perform oral sex on her mother. When Joker came in to bust up the party he hurried up to finish. The worst part of the whole thing, Joker realized as he was leaving was the 7-year-old boy. Ghostman had forced a cyanide capsule down his throat only minutes before the sexual assaults.

There the little guy lay on the floor where Ghostman had put him underneath discarded bed blankets, linens and clothes that had been strewn about.

Joker didn't want to judge Ghostman. That's because of all the blood that was on his own hands. Out of everything in his life that he did it was this incident that he thought about most. He watched Ghostman get dressed.

Ghostman looked at Joker "Man, you better getchu some of that. She was a virgin and I turnt that pussy out. She nutted while eating' her mutha pussy out. You should-"

PFFHHTT!! PFFHHTT!!

Joker blasted the daughter and the mother into hell. "Fuck both *of them dumb bitches! They da wife, daughter, son and grandfather of an Al Qaeda soldier! Let's roll."*

Prior to leaving they planted C-4 all throughout the structure. Their transportation squad returned, they detonated the bombs and turned the house into a raging inferno.

The Twin Towers

He felt a nudge on his elbow. It was Eden and Iani who had walked in on him Leah and the others.

"You sleep?" Iani asked, bending down to kiss him.

"Thinking," he stated with a smile.

"'Bout what?" Iani inquired.

"Afghanistan," he stated. "A long time ago."

He was tried though so eventually sleep won out.

CHAPTER THIRTY-SEVEN

Joker's Penthouse
Thursday Evening

First he had to deal with one, not two but *three* detectives from Chicago's Missing Case Squad and they played "nice…" at first.

Detective June Fahey.

Detective Kevin McDonald

And Detective Don Lutz.

June was a 5-foot 10 inch woman with an oval face, she was 38 but seemed to stay fit. She had dirty blond hair and she liked to keep spearmint chewing gum in her mouth.

Kevin McDonald was shorter than June, had a broad

chest, white hair although he was only 35, and was over-weight with a smoker's cough.

Don Lutz was raven-haired, he wore wire-rimmed glasses, and was over 6 feet tall with some bulk to him at 240 pounds.

They interviewed Joker Red first.

"What's your angle, Mr. Hodges?" Fahey probed as they stood in the hallway outside of his penthouse. "What do you do?"

"I'm a businessman," he told them. "Everything Is Everything, Inc. owner. We're involved in real estate, modeling recruitment, and private security services."

"Private security?" Fahey wanted to know more.

Joker nodded. "That's right."

"Did you see Jessika Cicero on the night in question?" Fahey inquired.

"Briefly," he answered. "She was plannin' a night out with a party of other models. After that I stayed home."

Leah and Uzenna were also interviewed. The detectives were allowed into Jessika's old apartment but were also informed that she was no longer living there. What they were not told was that Jessika, like hundreds of others now, had moved near her new job in Gary, Indiana-an underground strip club which was the front for one of EIE's crystal meth-amphetamine operations spots.

And then, subsequent to their departure, Vinnie Braga arrived with six of his killaz. Joker invited them inside of his penthouse where he assured Vinnie that they'd do everything possible to find Jessika.

"I'm hearin' whispers from the girls we spoke to that your man is involved up to his teeth," Vinnie coldly accused.

Joker sat down with Vinnie inside of his office-library and went back and forth with the Chicago crime syndicate under-boss. Joker *wanted* to lay it all out on the table, but he couldn't because he himself had already committed some extremely deceptive acts upon the Mafia-unforgivable acts. For example, the distribution of the so-called encrypted cellphones to Frank Braga and Vinnie Braga from Joker Red who was one of their most trusted criminal associated.

In addition to that deceit, Joker's justification for doing so, was his suspicion that a grand conspiracy to assassinate him and take over his empire was still being orchestrated. He really wanted to speak openly to Vinny about this but: *What if the Syndicate was involved?* He thought. That would defeat the purpose of distributing the flawed encryption technology. The Syndicate certainly had money, means and motive to overthrow Joker Red.

But Joker's gut was telling him that there was something much darker and more treacherous happening…Right inside of his own motherfucking circle. These dark forces had slaughtered comrade brothers he'd known for many years-Monk, Black N9NE, Big Chief, Fast Eddie Kane, Mustafa and Ground War. And, to further rip his heart out, those dark forces had murdered his children and wives-Louise/baby Stefanie, Melodie/baby Justin, Diane/baby Francesa and Julia/baby Afton.

In any event, Joker was suspecting Ghostman of being up yo something grimey but Joker had to be 100% sure first. And once he was reasonably certain. Joker Red had no intentions of warning Ghostman of his pending doom. Joker respected Ghostman Dinero's gangster too much for that. Ghostman had been shot multiple times, came out of a coma asking for a beer, he'd been beaten, tortured, stabbed and he'd survived all of it.

In the military, as an army Ranger, he was a monster. A killing machine. But so was Joker and all of the close knit EIE rogues but Ghostman was a sick *maniac*. No one knew it better than Joker Red.

"Why do I get the feeling here that you have a *'suspicion'* that you ain't sharing with me?" Vinnie asked, jarring Joker out of his private thoughts.

"I just don't know what to think Vinnie," Joker said, choosing his words very carefully. "You said you heard whispers about Ghostman…What am I s'posed to say to that?"

The he shook his head. "No…*You* said Ghostman. Not me. *You*. I said *'your man is involved'* to see what you'd say."

Joker Red nodded and sighed. "Yeah. How do I put this… Nothin' is more sensitive than fearing or the safety of someone you love, and I take it—or have heard—you have gotten particularly close to Jessica right?

A look of pure pain was etched across Vinnie's face. "Red, she was or is my mistress but-but…"

Joker knew Vinnie had a wife but that didn't matter. All gangsters had wives, or girlfriends, with women on the side. No big deal.

"But what, Vin?" Joker sat forward.

Then he looked up at him. "She just told me that she was

pregnant, man. And I decided to let her keep it," Vinnie revealed.

Joker Red saw that the man was on the brink of tears and clenched his teeth while shaking his head out of anger and sympathy for Vinnie.

"Now I didn't say Ghostman so you must have heard what I did," Vinnie stated once again. "Or…You must know something more."

"Believe me, Vinnie," Joker Red stated as he stood up and leaned up against the front of his desk so he could be face to face with Vinnie "The Butcher." "I see your pain and as a father who has lost wives and children…I also *feel* your pain. Don't let that pain make you look at me any different because I'm still me. And I wouldn't protect any of my men if they did foul play to women. Particularly to one of our own EIE girls. And everyone knows that the Braga's were particularly fond of our Italian-speaking girls—*Jessica, Carla, and Isabella especially.* And it was no secret that you have been seein' Jessika. Now…This baby you mentioned…My God, Vinnie. I'm at a loss…"

"Don't get in our way, Joker," Vinnie warned him face to face as he stood up. "Just don't."

"Take care, Vinnie."

Joker stared at his phone for several long moments after Vinnie exited. He pulled up Ghostman's number for a few seconds and then he just decided to turn the phone off altogether. Ghostman was on his own with that one. Joker wasn't going against his gut on it either.

CHAPTER THIRTY-EIGHT

The Boca Raton
Boca Raton, FL
Friday Evening

Joker Red, Tithi, Leah. Uzenna, Baby Joker I and his nanny Amelia met up with Coral, Ashley, Eden, Valerie, Iani, Brittani, the babies, Ceasar Breach, Casci and Bible Reed at the Boca Raton in Florida the next evening.

"Nina mentioned this mufucka," Joker said after he hugged and kissed his women and children. He turned to look at the front of the beautiful hotel. "Now y'all here, too."

"She's here now?" Iani wondered. "Nina I mean?"

"Nah, she was not long ago," he replied. "It's nice, though." He loved it.

They followed the bellboys in with all of their luggage, checked into their lavish suites and freshened up for dinner. Anyone who had knowledge of Boca Raton knew that it was originally built as a 100-room retreat by legendary architect Addison Mizner who ended up leaving his Mediterranean revival stamp all over Florida. Over the last century, the Boca Raton expanded up and out. It had recently been renovated with a well-spent $200 million and was not 1,000 room 200-acre resort which sat between half a mile of private beach and an Audubon Cooperative Sanctuary and divided by lake Boca. Everything about it was re-thought and reimagined for this brand-new chapter. This includes where Coral and Iani insisted on them eating at tonight: The Flamingo Grill, a chophouse with a staff in candy-pink blazers.

Within few short minutes a darling little waitress popped up at their table. She was dark chocolate color, her eyes were big, her hair very short and wavy like a boy and she couldn't have been any taller than five feet, 100 pounds, but she had a very nice shape. Lemon size breasts, a pert behind and she was just cute all over. Her name tag read *Mina* on it.

"¡Hola!" she greeted them. "I'm Mina, your waitress. May I get you-"

"Your phone number, sweetie!" Iani flirted with her. "Youse a dark chocolate Spanish mami, too? What's your nationality?"

"She's Cubana, Coral cut in. "Ain't you?"

Mina nodded, looking around at all the well-dressed women. Coreal was wearing a red Prada dress with a plunging neck and ack showing off a diamond Tiffany chain and bracelet set. All of the girls wore expensive designer dresses and they also donned diamond earrings, necklaces, rings and bracelets.

"One hundred percent Black-Cuban," Mina answered, blinking her long fashionable eyelashes at Joker Red. "May I get you-"

"Bottles," Joker cut her off with a kind smile. He moved over a little and the girls seated to this right did the same with humorous looks on their faces. "Sit with us, Mina," Joker invited her.

"Um, I don't think it's..." She hesitated.

Joker laid down on American Express Centurion "Black Card" which Mina instantly respected. "C'mon now, mamita. Just for a minute."

Mina smoothed out her candy-pink skirt and sat her sweet-smelling self down next to Iani.

"Y'all are so flamboyant!" Mina giggled.

"Flamboyant?" Leah asked. "Daddy?"

"Hm?" he replied as he scanned the menu.

"Show her flamboyant," Leah dared him.

"You do it," he shot back.

Leah stood up and shouted, *"Attention everyone!"*

The restaurant had at least 90 people in it. They looked at Leah like she was just another tipsy college girl in town during spring break.

"Everyone's bill is on us!" Leah yelled. "Eat up, drink

up!" People cheered, many yelling: "Here, here!" And holding drinks high.

The other waiters and waitresses came over to the EIE table where Leah gave the Mina the Black Card. "Tip each of the waiters and waitresses ten percent of the bill."

Joker Red saw Iani get Mina's phone number. "Cubana cutie…we ready to order," Joker told her.

Mina nodded and stood up. "Okay."

"Wines first," he said looking at the menu closely. "Get us the Malvasia Bianca and the Catarratto."

Mina nodded. "Those are white wines."

He nodded. "Yeah…We want the Barbera Barricato and Nero d'Avola. Those are my reds."

Mina smiled, impressed. "No one has asked for that before. Great selections. What else?"

"Italian girls?" He asked them. "Everyone want Italian food?"

They nodded.

Joker ordered some delicious dishes. "I'm tryna try the squash blossoms, crispy artichokes in salty salsa di accouche and…girls?"

Uzenna took over ordering. "We want the soft pizzas topped with taleggio cheese and black truffle. And, oh, mind you we have bodyguards and babies so extra pizza to be packaged up and ready to go. Oh, um, ten fried steaks to go as well."

"It all looks good," Leah said. "Let's all have the Spaghetti Alle Vongole and Caico Pepe."

Mina sent all of their orders to the kitchen first and she

went personally to retrieve the chilled bottles of wine. Since the wine collection they had at the Flamingo was award-winning and expensive Mina had to flag down a supervisor to escort her into the wine cellar.

"Whatta we got out there, a Miami Heat player?" the slim, pretty, female supervisor asked Mina after she located the wine EIE had ordered. "Those bottles are expensive," she noticed.

"He doesn't look like he plays pro ball but, Kim, he's the most beautiful man I've ever seen," Mina gushed as she pushed the wine cart back out.

While Mina place the wine in silver ice buckets, Kim and another manager called American Express who greenlight the purchases that were being made.

The wine was poured, the food arrived and the mood at the table was even better, Joker started right in on picking the girl's brains on what they'd learned and accomplished in Florida thus far.

"Land in Fort Lauderdale—not on short notice!" Uzenna said doing the cutthroat sign with her hand. "However, we did find the perfect mansion for us all to live in until our house are built."

"And we have located two plots land that are ideal for what we want built," Valerie reported. "North of here is Delray Beach. There's a plot of land there, just off the coastline."

"And the other?" Joker inquired.

"West Palm Beach," Iani answered. "It's all beach but below rock. The views of the ocean are breathtaking. We can build our own fortress-community and control who comes in the front. As for the rock cliff outback they'd have to be a daredevil to attempt scaling it. And we can have and operate helicopters there."

He pulled it up on his laptop. First he looked at Google Maps.

"I like the distance from Miami," he said.

He pulled it up on Google Earth maps and located the beach and cliff edges as well.

"Price," he said.

"Four million?" Uzenna nearly ducked as she said it as if he was going to throw something at her because it was so high.

"We're making twenty million a month right now on average," he revealed to them for the first time. "Trust me when I say, a lot is being poured into overheard, the air base, government, weapons and more. But, okay, but it."

They finished up their meal and returned to the hotel.

CHAPTER THIRTY-NINE

West Palm Beach Villa
Saturday Afternoon

The very next day Joker Red was able to apply for and be granted leave inside of an office complex. He had the entire four floor building to himself and immediately contacted Nina and Lieutenant Sampson Gates about the location for his new intelligence service. Or Central Intelligence Network (CIN).

"Florida's as good a place as any I guess," Gates said. "Text me the address and expect a team of tech guys to show up Monday to get started."

At the Boca Raton, Uzenna and the other girls were having lunch with Joker when she asked him, "Why'd you tell us we make twenty million per month now?" Uzenna wondered.

He thought it over. "Don't you wanna know?" he asked.

"It's scary number," Leah said.

He nodded. "Yeah. And someone's trying to kill us over it. Youse need to hear how ugly the shit is gotten."

The comment made all of them worry.

"What's going on, baby?" Brittani asked outright.

He stood up after he was done. "Let's pack up this luggage and move it into that Fort Lauderdale mansion y'all was talkin' bout.

"No," Uzenna said. "It's a West Palm Beach mansion. Not far from the land we'll be buying and building upon. Wanna stop by and see it?"

He declined. "Y'all got it. C'mon now cuz I haveta get back and prepare for a mission." But they later talked him into seeing it anyway.

JOKER JUMPED OUT OF THE GRAY STRETCH HUMMER AND whistled after taking one look at the mansion. It was a spectacular Mediterranean style villa with the price tag of $8.5 million. Joker Red shook his head at his wives because the place was a palace. It was 28,893 square feet with 10 bedrooms, 10 full bathrooms, 3 partial bathrooms, an indoor swimming pool, full gym, two stories, seven car garage bays, tennis courts, basketball courts, a first floor master bedroom. 8- to 10-foot-high ceilings, a covered lanai, cabana, breakfast nook, a covered balcony and so much more.

"Who buys a house like this and doesn't live in it 24/7?" Joker wondered around as they walked inside through the front door.

Iani handed him a tabloid magazine story about a white billionaire businessman who was getting divorced from his R&B superstar wife following allegations of her having an affair with her plastic surgeon.

"Apparently this house is one of many assets the couple are splitting down the middle," Iani explained. "It was one the mutually agreed to lease out, so we have it for six months at sixty thousand per month plus utilities, insurance, security, etcetera."

"Breach," Joker called him over.

"Boss?" Breach responded. He was an icy blue eyed white man with a deep tan. A marine sniper and infantryman during *Operation: Iraqi Freedom and Enduring Freedom*. After the wars he went back to work for Blackwater, a PMC (E.G. Private Military Corporation).

"Get Gates on the phone," Joker told him, handing him a burner, "Tell him I need eighteen killaz here, six will work on eight-hour shifts, to protect my family, armed escort, everything. I need 'em now."

Breach handled the security set up.

Fortunately, the house came with furnishings, beds, lighting, and so forth. That's what had stood out to Iani and Uzenna when they first looked at the luxury listings. The house came fully equipped.

He walked in the master bedroom and was impressed. It was 21 feet by 24 feet with 8-foot-high ceilings between it, sitting area, and bath, "This is what I'm talkin' bout. I'm gonna love this house, this room, being in here chilling with y'all," he smiled "C'mere, China Doll witcha fine ass."

"What?" She was walking past him when he caught her around the waist. He rubbed his nose all in the crook of her neck and inhaled her sweetness. "What're you doin'? Oh-mmm," she started to moan.

He feather kissed her pink lips and hungrily devoured her mouth in front of everybody. She melted against him, the kiss seeming to go on and on, forever. Then sensing that Ceasar, Breach, Bible, and Casci were nearby she pushed him away.

"Whatchu bein' all shy about?" he asked her. "Casci, Ceasar, Bible, and Breach all gone."

White China looked around and the EIE personnel had already exited the room. The only ones there were Joker, Coral, Uzenna, Ashley, Leah, Eden, Valerie, Iani, Brittani, and Tithi.

The babies were in the living room the Amelia, the other nannies and the henchman.

"Uzenna, *undress*," Joker commanded as he sat in a big black overstuffed recliner chair. "Matter fact, all of you undress. If you wanna play…"

He led by example. He took off all of his clothes and the women saw that his dick was already swollen and pulsating with fury.

"Here?" Ashley said, running a hand back through her long brunette hair. She removed her stylish glasses.

"Now?" the slender blond, Eden, answered. But even as she spoke she peeled off her gray Bruce Springsteen shirt and wiggled out of her skirt, allowing it to puddle at her bare feet. She wore no bra her breasts were pink topped with nipples that looked like pink gumdrops.

Uzenna was not hesitant to get undressed as her husband stared a lustful hole into all of them.

"Have you been a good girl, wife?" he asked her.

Oh my god, Uzenna thought. *He's gonna whoop me again.* She instantly felt her uvula pulsate and the lips of her pussy emitted cream drops.

"I been good," she said in a small voice.

"Come lay across my lap," he ordered her. "The rest of y'all sit down and prepare them hot wet pussies for sex with your husband."

Uzenna obeyed and laid across Joker's lap. "Please don't hurt me…I been so good."

"You healed up fast I see," he said, rubbing his hand over her warm honey-colored, tattooed buttocks. "I don't have any reason to spank your ass…but I see you're wet already."

"I am?" she acted like she didn't know. She reached a hand underneath her and stuck two fingers inside of her pink peach. She got up half way and rubbed those pussy soaked fingers all up under his nose and lips, "Oh! I see whatchu talkin' 'bout now."

He picked her up and carried her to bed. She needed that fine ass and pussy eaten. She was juicing for real now. As soon as she hit the bed, however, Iani turned her over onto her back and got on top of her, covering her like a hungry vampire. She wanted her little sister very bad.

Iani kissed her, grabbed her luscious breasts, twisting her nipples, pinching them hard. The two girls were humping into each other, finally scissoring their legs and grinding their excited pussies together. Soon they were holding onto each other for dear life as their clits kissed and their wet snatches gushed warm girl juices out. The room started to smell like sex already.

"I love you, Eden," Joker said as he kissed all up and down, between the blue-eyed blonde's slender tanned thighs, He knew this made her pussy wet. "It's all dark pink inside… it's *mad* horny, huh?"

"Hurry, oh, please!" Eden pleaded, pushing her dripping slit toward his slavering mouth. "Please, oh, god, suck my pussy, oh! I love you…ooouuu!" she moaned at first contact.

He gave her what she wanted, plunging his long, stiffened tongue deep up into the beautiful girl's twat, moaning with pleasure as he lapped up all her gushing honey. For fifteen minutes he ate that pussy.

Then he turned to Valerie, pulling her away from Tithi. He laid her out and hungrily went to tasting her fruits. For several minutes he used slow, lewdly teasing strokes of his tongue inside of the tall blonde's pussy, licking the warm wet walls clean of their delicious juices. Then he began to fuck his tongue in and out of her tight slit. Faster and faster he tongued her until Valerie was grinding her hips madly and screaming with erotic joy beneath him….

"Damn you taste good!" he complimented her. His eye

caught White China again. She was between Tithi's legs fingering and tonguing her wet gash. "There you are…and all these fly ass tattoos y'all poppin' up with."

He didn't want to disturb Tithi so he licked and kissed all of Coral's hot naked flesh. He opened up her asscheeks and slurped up and down the warm crack. Licking in wet circles and twists around the small orifice of her asshole. He edged his lips ever closer to her wet sticky cunt below. She smelled exceptionally delectable.

Coreal spread her legs as wide as they would ho and got on her knees, exposing her turgid labia in their full glory, like a new-blown rose, watching the lips expand and contract eagerly before his thrilling oral plunge between them. He filled his nostrils with the scent of Coral's sweet Chinese pussy, torturing himself. He knew that pussy scent drove him crazy.

He plastered his face into her pussy and tongue fucked her like a maniac, his nose all smashed up against her asshole. But she smelled like her strawberry body wash from the Philosophy fragrance collection. He anus looked like a brownish-beige asterisk.

First Eden, then Valerie and Coral…He'd looked around and seen Iani devouring her own sister. Coral taking out her hunger on Tithi. Now, Leah had Ashley's legs all the way back, while she planted her face inside of her sweet pie. And Brittani and Valerie were now locked into a red hot 69 which had them both winding and grinding, moaning and groaning in their own world.

When he sat at the head of the bed Eden came to him and

impaled her wet gripping cavern onto the big plum-sized head of his pole. He immediately grabbed her dreamy asscheeks and looked into her eyes.

"This whatchu need, Eden baby?" he whispered hotly. This is how it always was.

She started the ride, using his juicy light skinned cucumber to touch her in spots that only he could. She looked so sexy as she hopped up and down. She would get flat on her feet with her legs spread wide, her hands behind her and she would work that dick by swiveling her hips. He started at her wine-colored nipples and drooled because he wanted to suck them.

"Oooouuu, Daddy, you love that, huh?" she whispered swear pouring down her lovely body. "Fuck that pussy! It's white, tight, it smells great…"

She leaned forward, kissing him, fucking that big veiny dick in and out of her. She rode him so good and hard that the other girls stopped what they were doing in the orgy to watch.

They loved when Eden got like this because she was usually so demure. But right now she had Joker, where she wanted him. "Don't move, Daddy!" she cried as she fucked that huge pole all the way in and then the nearly all the way out. "Please don't Move! My Black dick right now. Take this wet ass white pussy!"

She controlled him even through all the squishy sounding orgasms she had. Her energy was incredible!

"Do it, Daddy…" she begged. "Buss that nut all up in me…gimme another baby girl. Oooouuuuuu, I feel that shit hardening…go, Daddy, wet it all up in my stomach…ohhh, shit, cum in me! Like that! My cum! My Daddy! My dick! My big black dick! Ummm, it feels good! So hot and wet. Soak me with it! I want another daughter, Daddy!"

He had cum so good and so hard that he was having a hard time catching his breath! He kissed her and asked for water! Once he was able to drink he was good.

He looked around. "Y'all done? Damn, Eden!"

Valerie and the others shook their heads. "Cuz I'm juiced up," he said. "My dick ain't goin to sleep for hours." He was still hard as hell.

So they all had a wonderful orgy for hours.

CHAPTER FORTY

Chicago O'Hare
Wednesday Afternoon

"Valoria Pincse," Nina told him as they were driven away from Chicago O'Hare Airport. Nina had arranged for them to travel in a Mercedes-Benz Sprinter to appease Joker who appreciated the leg room and the luxury. "Pronounced Pink-See spelled P-I-N-C-S-E. But that name is fake-as is her passport."

Joker Red was all ears. "Fake U.S. Passport?"

"That, too," she said. "And I mean it's so good as fake that it got our attention. Information-sharing inside of the intelligence community has gotten pretty good so Homeland informed us that Interpol suspected an Albanian Mafia group of manufacturing fake European passports. We wanted to see them and what we found was alarming. They truly are fakes and if the Albanian Mafia-"

"They could be sold to a terrorist who's on a no-fly list," Joker finished for her.

"Not just in Europe where we have many interests but here," she went on emphatically.

"If they could do such a superior job on the European Passports…then counterfeiting the U.S. passport is next on the list. And they did it."

"What's your real name?" Joker asked.

"Victoria Linze, L-I-N-Z-E," Nina revealed.

"Fuck me," Joker said as he read the CIA file on Victoria Linze from the laptop Nina passed him.

"What?" Nina asked.

"Tithi," he said. "It says here that Linze has been involved in the opening of tattoo shops through legitimate proxies. Tithi got a tiger cubs tattoo with Aconite plants, flowers and all."

"The Aconite flower, huh?" Nina looked at him with caution. "She's Indian—a Hindu, right?"

He nodded. "Yeah. So?"

Nina had to warn him. "Not saying that she'd do it. But there have been cases where Indian women poison their husbands for infidelity and abuse."

"Oh yeah?" Joker laughed, thinking about his little Tithi doing that.

"Yeah," she nodded. "So…this tiger tattoo."

"She mentioned how Honey B hooked her up with an

Albanian tattoo artist," Joker said, becoming visibly irate. "My enemy? Touchin' my woman's feet?"

"Her *feet*?" Nina asked him. "Okay I'm baffled."

Joker took a deep breath. "You ever see the movie *Pulp Fiction* with Samuel L. Jackson and John Travolta?"

"The foot massage incident or something?" That's an old movie," she reminded him. "They are feet. Why get mad over *feet* that's what I'm saying. Be mad that there's other sinister shit going on."

Joker knew she just wouldn't understand.

"What if he puts a tattoo on her booty?" Nina asked him. "What's worse?"

"The foot tattoo," he said.

Nina paused. "I mean he's touching your woman's *behind*. Her anus is there. Her vagina and inch or so later. All that goin' on."

Joker shook his head. "When a man kisses, caresses, massages, tattoos a woman's foot she's looking down at him, he's looking up at her. As her feet are being touched her pussy juices. There are an insane amount of erogenous zones or sex nerves that shoot directly to a woman's clitoris and nipples. And a man that knows a woman understands that being on a knee looking up is sexy to her. That leg is there, the eye contact, all the physicality that comes with seduction."

"So, I take it you have a foot fetish," Nina smiled.

"A pretty female feet fetish," he corrected her.

"Toe sucking?"

"Of course."

"Do you smell them?"

"Damn right and they smell clean," he said. "Like Eden... even when she comes out of that red bottom, she wore all day she smell good even though she wants a shower first."

"She thinks she's *sweated* in her shoe and wants to wash first!" Nina told him.

"She *has* sweated but that's *her*," he explained. "I wanna smell *her*."

Nina laughed. "Men and fetishes."

"I love the scent of pussy," he admitted. "It don't have to be sweaty," I just love the smell. And females absolutely *love* to let us smell them."

Nina nodded. "For millions of years men and women both have been attracted to sexual scent."

"You act like I have a *clinical* fetish, but I only like pretty female feet," he stated accusatorially.

"It's just something I don't understand," she said, shrugging a little. "It's cute though." "You ever smell your man's pillow or T-shirt he was wearin'?" Joker inquired.

She smiled. "Oh, yeah! I like wearing my man's T-shirt... and boxers he wore."

"Okay, I like smelling panties my women wear," he said. "And if you smellin' a man's T-shirt...he *sweated* in it. His armpits was in it." Are you weird fo liking it-not to mention his dirty boxers?"

She giggled. "You shoulda been a trial lawyer."

"Do you have pretty feet?" he asked her.

"I have *beautiful* feet," she nodded.

"How do you know?"

"Because I asked my niece on Facebook about a color I was wearing to her graduation and next thing I knew my feet were all over Facebook," she explained. "There were some men who offered me fifty dollars for new foot photos."

"Hm," Joker looked down at her feet and, as usual, she wore field boots. "Wish I could see those pictures."

The spoke more extensively about Victoria Linze, AKA Valoria, during the ride to the Towers.

"You know she's been smuggling a lot of Albanian men into country," Nina said, showing him a report written by a U.S. Border Patrol agent. "Two Albanian men were apprehended at the U.S.-Mexico border in Tijuana and one of them had an address to report to in Chicago."

Joker looked at her expectantly. "What's the mufckin' address?" he demanded.

"None can find it," she quipped. "But it's in Little Village."

Joker shook his head. "Nah man. These mufuckas is comin' through the backdoor...here to Chi-Town? Little Village? We have a lot of cash flowin' through there."

They reached the Towers and went to the War Room. Joker texted Tithi and asked her to come down.

"I need y'all to run a GPS track on Ghostman's phone all last week," Joker requested. "Gates' tech team will need more time before the CIN is all set up. But I'm tryna see where he mighta disposed of Jessika's body."

"Whattaya gonna do with the intel if you find anything?" Nina wanted to know. "He's an EIE soldier."

"Yeah, I know." Joker replied. "A damned good one. But if he did this...it ain't somethin' I'm condoning, And if I confront him with it he'll know I know. And I'll tell him he's out. And that I'm passing the find over to the Syndicate to prevent a war. That's all I can do and prepare for any reaction. I don't fear that mufucka."

Nina sent a text message to the CIA.

"I'm struck that you'd do that," Nina said.

He nodded. "He's a friend but…My children and wives were murdered. My comrades. And I'm starting to believe my gut feeling. I just don't have all the facts yet. Somethin' treacherous is boiling behind my back. So…This girl Jessika is the mistress of Vinnie Braga. No! No!"

Joker was pissed. This was bad.

"Calm down now," Nina said quietly. "Shh. What is it?"

"I know him," Joker admitted. "I know for a fact…We were exterminators over there. Al Qaeda, Taliban, we killed them and stole their heroin and weapons. Fifty percent of everything was sent to EIE HQ in Brooklyn. I've seen him rape and beat women. Literally, he *cannibalized* them. Bite them until their flesh comes off. He put a bullet in their heads like sheep. I've heard a lot worse about him. He's a serial killer."

"We'll find the Cicero girl," Nina assured him not wanting to hear anymore. "Christ!"

He let it drop but couldn't play the fool while looking into the mirror. For his entire life he lived by the gut and now he knew. And knowledge is power. A super-power. *Sometimes rose-colored glasses could hide the red flags.*

"Glasses hiding what?" Nina inquired.

"Huh?" He didn't realize that he was talking loud. "Nothin', just a saying I believe in that I heard my mama say long ago. It stuck. Something rose colored glasses could hide the red flags."

She looked at him through slitted eyes saying, "I'll remember it."

"Yeah, baby. You do that," he told her. "I just know Ghost-man. I've done shit with him in the Middle East. I mean we had them Al Qaeda niggas scared…but he looked me dead in the face and lied about Jessika. I coulda concocted some solid shit-even brought The Butcher a innocent body to cover it up…cuz Ghostman is important to everything. I know where da bone are wit da Ghostman, and he sure know where mine at."

"What's different?" the dark-skinned CIA lady asked.

"Red flags and roses," he responded as they prepared to speak to Tithi the Indian doctor. "Whether in Brooklyn streets, Chicago streets, Kabul villages, war zones, a fist fight, whatever problem you got it won't get solved if you lack knowledge cuz knowledge is *power* not coincidence. A coinci-dence is a lie, a shortcut that'll getchu killed. And what we have is exactly that. Albanians bein' smuggled into the U.S. from Mexico…had a Chicago address no one could locate? What's that?"

"Coincidence?" she asked more than answered. "In the briefing we spoke about that, but your emotion, your anger, and passion adds a lot more than I could get across. I mean I know a border control agent seen the address written on the back of a dry-cleaning receipt and…"

"Valoria or Victoria is a force to be reckoned with," he

mentioned. "She's a heavy hitter. A boss bitch. Trust my guy. Imma street nigga and I'd bet anything that she paid another agent to scrub the file clean of addresses, phone numbers and so forth. For all we know she also has Interpol in her pocket."

"That's possible," Nina agreed.

"Fuck right it is. She got the attention of the CIA right?" he stated and she nodded. "You said...didn't you say Homeland Security Administration told CIA that Interpol suspects the Albanians for makin' fake European passports?"

"Yup," she replied. "And we already know a lot about the *Albania Besa Mafia*. They make Albert Anastasia's U.S. Mafia, by comparison look like The Boy Scouts of America— Rainbow carrying Eagle Scoutmaster heading up the front of the boys! *Ha! Ha! Ha!*"

She was laughing so hard that she made Joker laugh.

"If the Rainbow carryin' ass Eagle Scouts up front," he dropped humorously,

"then them gay ass Catholic Cardinals and Bishops is headin' up the back talkin' 'bout *'where them First Grade Boys at!' Ha! Ha! Ha! Ha!* You crazy, Nina."

"If we had a TV show and called them Catholic Cardinals and Bishops out like that...our show would get canceled!" she grinned.

"Fuck cancel culture and every mufucka whoever been a part of it," he said serious as a heart attack. "C'mon, let's handle this."

Play time was over.

CHAPTER FORTY-ONE

The War Room

Tithi entered the warm room and saw Nina seated at the furthest left end of the long conference table while Joker sat at the furthest right end of the table. Nina was taking advantage of a nutritious meal by eating a grain cereal, a high protein homemade health mix, sliced bananas, honey, and goat's milk in a large bowl.

Tithi held a ceramic bowl in her hands that was covered by aluminum foil which she removed and sat next to Joker. Inside were ten pieces of fried salmon. She went into the kitchen, poured orange juice, retrieved plates and silverware, and brought them back out to the war room.

Nina and Joker Red were having a good laugh when she returned and made three plates of the fish. "What?" Tithi smiled. "What's so funny?"

"Nothin'," he said.

She shrugged and cut a chunk of the delicious-looking salmon with his fork and held it up for him to eat. "Here, Daddy. I made your favorite fish."

He smiled and blocked her from feeding him. "That's not my favorite fish."

"Huh?" She frowned.

Nina was laughing her ass off.

Tithi looked at him through slit eyes. "Are y'all high?"

He shook his head. "Nah, babe, nobody high."

"Eat then," she said. "It's favorite. You told me many times..."

"Here, baby, you eat it with me," he said taking the fork and holding it up to her mouth.

"What's going on here?" Tithi stood up and stared Nina down.

"Calm down," Joker told her. "We were jokin'-fuckin witchu. Callin' you Lil Miss Aconite and shit."

"That's not funny," she said as a text came through on her phone. She quickly answered it with one of her own. Several more texts followed which she read but didn't reply to. "So why you call me here? I have to run to the hospital once more."

Joker observed her closely. "Why? You quit."

Nina moved nearer so they could all speak in quieter voices. "The tattoo you have. You told your husband here that an Albanian man Honey B knows referred you to him correct?"

"Is that a crime?" Tithi asked.

"I'm sorry but, no first off," Nina explained. "Secondly, I'm not law enforcement. I'm an Intelligence Agent."

Tithi nodded as Joker pulled the plate of fish closer to him. He grabbed the fork, scooped up some of the Salmon and Nina got up quickly saying, *"Don't eat that, Red!"* she snapped like lightning.

Joker stared at her strangely but put the fork down slowly. "You serious?"

"Gimme the phone," Nina demanded.

Tithi relinquished the phone but shouted, "What the hell is this crazy bitch doing, Joker?!"

"Bring the plate over here, Joker," Nina said sitting on the table to the right of where Tithi sat.

Joker picked up the plate, scooped up a small bite of the fish and looked at Tithi. "You wouldn't poison me, Tee, would you?" he asked her.

"This woman is crazy!" Tithi said angrily.

"Then you'll eat it," Joker said, hoping Nina was wrong.

Tithi nodded yes. "I have no reason to. It is utterly ridiculous that I'd have any desire to harm the father of my child. I am a doctor. *Do no harm* is in my oath."

He brought the food up to her mouth but at the last second, she turned her head.

"I'm not hungry," she said, knowing it was over.

"Is she really pregnant?" Nina asked, crossing her arms.

Joker nodded. "Yeah. But she's a doctor. It could all be fake! What—why, Tee? The three million stashed in the Manhattan loft. The gold bars in the Caymans?"

Tithi was tight lipped. Nina was glad she trusted her gut. And his, too.

From out of nowhere Joker had balled up a fist, cocked it back to Detroit and brought it back full speed ahead to Tithi's face! He knocked her backwards off of chair making her tumble over with her stomach's contents spewing out of her mouth from the impact.

"You ain't gonna wanna be here for the rest!" he growled. Tithi was unconscious for a full minute. "I'll clean all of this up."

Tithi was groaning and crying as she came to and struggled to stand up.

Nina asked him, "Get everything out of here so we know what we're dealing with?"

What neither of them knew was that Tithi had a trick shot. She deployed a "mace grenade" in their direction and it exploded with eye-burning and skin searing precision! She stumbled to the front door and threw the percussion grenade behind her so it exploded where Joker and Nina were!

As Joker and Nina had both dove for cover at the first moment they saw or heard the first grenade hit like they'd learned in basic training many years ago. Joker thought of how he had trained all of his own women to survive in non-survivable situations. This had been one of those situations and Tithi had bought herself some valuable time.

When he realized the grenades, she'd thrown weren't incendiary or destructive he got to his feet, and led Nina out of the front door. They were both coughing but, as soldiers, they were no strangers to mace, pepper sprays and such chemicals. Therefore, they needed very little time to recoup.

"You get outta here!" Joker shoved her in the direction of the stairwell.

"What are you doin'!" Nina asked.

"I know where she's going!" He ran down the one flight of stairs and out to the front parking lot.

"There!" Nina yelled, pointing at a black Chrysler 300 with a bald-headed white man driving it and another dark haired white man in the backseat. Nina had seen Tithi jump inside of it before it sped off!

Joker was already on his phone. He texted Blackout to send all available EIE to Ghostman's. He also texted Vinnie.

"Red?" Vinnie answered.

"Send every gun you got!" Joker snapped. "Meet me at Ghostman's!"

"You got it," Vinnie didn't hesitate.

Joker shook his head and jumped inside of his Bugatti Chiron. "You need to leave! You were never here! He barked at Nina."

Nina knew there was nothing more she could do. "You have no tac gear, no weapons…" she pointed out.

He popped open a behind-the-front-passenger's seat stash and removed two M5's, double Glocks and a dozen hand-grenades, "Plus, my squad's on the way."

He fired up the engine and roared out of the parking lot, tires burning rubber.

On The Highway

CHAPTER FORTY-TWO

On The Highway

The Chrysler 300 was no match for the lightning-fast Bugatti. Joker Red *wanted* to put the shit together piece by piece in his mind but couldn't. Especially not while driving at 170mph.

When he spotted the Chrysler 300, he slowed down and put his headset in. He got Meth Man Ace on the line and filled him in on everything.

"Group text all of EIE what I told you, son!" Joker told him. "So they know, cuz they on the way to blast holes in this mufucka! And these Albanian niggas!"

"Doin' it now!" Ace said. "Be careful out there, son!"

Joker slid down both windows, readied one of the M5's

and sped up. There was no way he was gonna let Tithi live after this shit.

The Chrysler hit the highway and Joker was right on it. He planned to drive up along its passenger's side and light it up from his driver's seat because that was his strong side since he was right-handed. He knew the men inside had to be armed so he needed to be careful.

When he was thirty yards out, he could see that Tithi was still seated behind the driver. He sped up!

He sped up! He brought the Bugatti within ten or fifteen yards from the desired target position! He sat the nose of the M5 across his driving arm and just let loose on the Chrysler 300!!

B-R-R-R-A-A-A-T-T-T!!!

B-R-R-R-A-A-A-T-T-T!!!

B-R-R-T-A-A-A-T-T!!!

Automatic gunfire ripped and peppered the rear window and right rear side of the bulky black sedan! He kept firing like a madman! Hitting the car!

B-R-R-R-A-A-A-T-T-T!!!

B-R-R-R-A-A-A-T-T-T!!!

B-R-R-R-A-A-A-T-T-T!!!

He had to switch guns. As he did so he didn't see the Dodge Charger creeping up on his blindside! One of the Albanian men inside of the Chrysler, the passenger, stuck his AR-15 out of the shattered rear window and returned fire at the Bugatti!

Joker cocked that bitch up into the gear and sped up! This was the chance he was waiting for! He shot past the Chrysler and opened fire! The driver caught a volley of rounds to the arm and neck, causing him to lose control of the vehicle! It crashed, rolled over several times and turned into a ball of fire!

"Yeah!! "he roared. "You bitch! "He forged on ahead and slowed down. He pulled off at the Winthrop exit and just as he did the Bugatti was hit by a thunderous spray of M-16 and AK-47 slugs! Unfortunately, the Bugatti was not bullet proof like the other fleets of vehicles. He had because he was not only hit but, like the Chrysler 300, he lost control!

The car spun into a 360 circle and flipped twice down into a ravine!

The hired hittaz inside of the black Charger slowed make sure that Joker Red was surely dead. Since the multi-million dollar Bugatti had turned into a huge fireball the passenger was shouting at the driver in their native Albanian Gheg dialect to "*MOVE! HE'S DEAD! HE'S DEAD!*"

A woman had slowed to have a look from inside of her Toyota Camry. She was horrified to no end when the man on the passenger's side of the Charger cursed at her, aimed his deadly machine gun directly her way, and pulled the trigger. But the magazine was empty! She slammed on the gas of her car and never looked back! She would later tell the police that the men involved in the highway shootings were white-Albanian.

When the police asked how she knew she would say, "I have Albanian friends who speak the Indo-European language of the Albanians and they have two major dialects: *Gheg* and *Tosk*. I'm a hundred percent positive."

At the crash site the Albanian men had taken off as well.

Other passerby-motorists-had pulled over to the shoulder, hopped out their vehicles to see if there was anything they could do to help…but the Bugatti was a coffin on fire.

To Be Continued…

Did you enjoy the read?

Let us know how much by leaving us a review on Amazon and Goodreads.

PREVIEW

Keep reading for a preview of…

Coldhearted

By Lou Garden Price Sr.

PART ONE

Blood Stains and Broken Trust

CHAPTER ONE

Newport Gardens Apartments
Brownsville, NY
Monday 3:00 AM

Five-year-old Sage Michael Thomas peeked through the slightly open door where he thought he might locate his mother, father, or maybe even both. He had been asleep on his pissy smelling airbed in the back of the apartment when he was awakened by several roaches crawling on his face, neck, and bare chest. Then, to top it off, a mouse had ran across his legs. They were all licking remnants of the peanut butter and jelly he had eaten the night before.

He was starving all over again and he was in luck because

there they both were, on that old nasty brown living room sofa. Daddy was seated with his pants down and Mommy's face was moving up and down in his lap – making wet eating noises. Well, to Sage it sounded like eating noises…

It was only 3:00 AM so it was still dark outside. That meant it was dark inside because Con Edison had turned out the lights. Sage heard Mommy and Daddy arguing about it the day before. In fact, Daddy had whooped her ass really bad. Afterwards, Daddy had given Sage the peanut butter and jelly to eat, no bread.

Sage knew not to bother Mommy while she was "eating" Daddy so he just tried to see better. The only light he had to see with was from two of those tall glass candles depicting pagan sketches of the so called *Virgin Mary* crying. Or *weeping* as the Catholics put it.

The faint candlelight flickered, casting a silhouette image of his mother slurping on his father, Big Kato. Arnesha, his mother, was still a hot piece at eighteen even though she'd had a five year old son at an early age and a dope habit. But that didn't matter because when she walked through the hood, niggas was still staring at that chocolate ass she was packing in them jeans. She was bad as fuck.

When Lindsey Lohan, Demi Lovato, and half of them bitches in Hollywood turn dopefiend, pillhead, alcoholic, or whatever, niggas still wanted to fuck them hos. The 'hood ain't no different except skin color and economic status. But the pussy remains the same.

"Arnesha! What – who da fuck was dat?" came from the

startled voice from the funky sofa he was getting his dick and balls licked on. "I thought you said no one else was here!"

"Don't just stand out there, boy," came the actual voice of his father from the far left. "C'mere!" Sage, confused, walked past the strange man on the sofa who Sage had initially thought was his father, wondering why Mommy was on her knees eating from him. Sage only wore a pissy pamper which his father took off of him, trashed it, and put on a fresh one.

"Can we go to another room?" the strange older Black man asked Arnesha in a whisper. "I'm so close."

"C'mon, baby," she said, starting to get up.

"Nah, bitch," Kato growled from where he sat in the kitchen. "Finish toppin' that greasy ass nigga off right there!" he demanded coldly.

"But the lil nigga," the trick protested, but only for a moment.

"Pay attention to me, honey," she said as she took him back into her warm wet mouth. She was so thick, her chocolate titties were out and he held her head as he hardened fully again. *"Mmm! Glbb!* Mmm...*"*

"You see ya mama, son?" Kato whispered into Sage's little ear so that neither she nor her trick could hear him narrate what was happening. "She earnin' money for the lights to come on... and so you can have some milk, bread, eggs, and cereal. You want Captain Crunch?"

Sage nodded while keeping an eye on his Mother.

"See, son," Kato continued on. "Truth is, I went to jail and come home to a dopefiend whore. She tells me you prolly ain't even mine. That made me feel so evil I wanted to kill her and you."

Kato, whose real name was Titus White, was no slouch in the streets, but Arnesha was a ho and that reflected on him. Ever since they were both in the 7th Grade together they'd been in love. But when she'd gotten pregnant that changed everything. That pressure, coupled with the fact that neither of them were the brightest students to come out of Wingate High School, Kato had resorted to selling crack. Naturally, that eventually landed him in jail.

During his stay on Rikers Island, Arnesha had began popping Zannies and OxyContin's. Not long after that, she'd started snorting heroin. To support her growing habit she'd sold pussy. Subsequently, Kato was released to see her and Sage living in complete and total squalor at the notorious Noble Drew Ali Plaza Projects on New Lots and Mother Gaston Avenues in Brownsville.

In any event, Kato was a fearless stickup kid by trade so it didn't take long for him to move Arnesha and Sage into Newport Gardens Apartments on Lott and Rockaway Avenues. It was around that time when Kato's probation had been violated and he'd been returned to Rikers Island for a few months.

This time, when he was released, the streets were laughing even harder behind his back because another man had emerged as a possible father for Sage. Now, this ho not only fucked half the whole Brownsville but now Sage was "probably not" his son?

The sticky wet slurping sounds continued.

Glbb! Glbb! Mmm! The loud breathing and her sloppy sucking and moaning sounds had now filled the entire room. The candlelights seemed to burn brighter. *Glbb! Glbb! Mmmm, Mmmm!*

SWWOOOSSSHHH!! A sound similar to a wire hanger slicing through the air at 100 mph. And then, right behind that a flat: TTHHUUMMPP! sound. Something heavy hitting the floor behind the sofa. But Arnesha was currently throating her trick as if her life depended on it. She thought her son had dropped something and ignored it. All that mattered was the dick in her mouth and the $50 he had paid. She was trying to finish him off and get herself a fix.

However, Arnesha felt the moisture of a misty like spray hitting her face and forearm as if it were raining and a window was open nearby. Then, she realized that one second the tricks member was raging hard and then the next he was instantly flaccid. "What the hell, man?!" She complained.

She looked up at his face and she jumped backwards, screaming as she fell onto her ass, knocking over the littered coffee table! The trick's entire head was missing!

To her left stood Big Kato, a large 6 foot 2 inch, 240 pound young man with curly hair and no facial hair. He wielded a long, sharp, machete in his right hand with blood leaking off the blade. Arnesha trembled and screamed bloody murder when she looked over to her right and saw the trick's head, its eyes open, staring directly at her!

"OH, MY FUCKIN GOD!!!" She yelled and then started screaming.

"Shut yo ho ass up!!" Kato boomed, pointing the machete down at her.

He turned to Sage and for an extended, silent, moment he stared at him. Perhaps he'd contemplated killing him. Kato had lost it. He had the look of a madman in his eyes.

"Every man needs his dignity, Sage," Kato declared to the boy. "Remember dat."

He used his cellphone to pull up Youtube. Once he was filming himself he said, "Aight this must be how the white folks, school shooters, and terrorists do it huhn? Well, everybody, I just beheaded this dirty mufucka... as he was gettin' head by a ho I thought I loved. Take a look..."

He showed the world the decapitated head as best as he could with the darkness in the room. "See? This is my machete, my kill. This is my... I think he's my son. This bitch is his mother – a whore. She fucked all of my boys, I'm a laughingstock. A man needs his fuckin' dignity. So this is how I'm goin' out."

With that, he sat the phone down so it could record his next move. Then, he turned the machete on Arnesha...

When the cops arrived, from the 73rd precinct, he lunged at them with the machete raised in one hand while carrying Sage with the other, as a human shield! He was cut down immediately with a burst of semi-automatic gunfire!

"Hold your fire!!" a yell came.

"Hold your fire!!" someone repeated.

"He has a child!!" a ESU Sergeant bellowed.

Cops discovered that the child had also been shot and that

sent everyone into an even greater panic! Sage was rushed to the hospital!

But not even the Youtube video could have prepared them for the shock and horror of what was inside of the apartment.

Available Now
on all online retail book platforms!!

OTHER BOOKS BY

URBAN AINT DEAD

Tales 4rm Da Dale

The Hottest Summer Ever

Hittin' Licks For The Holidays: Atlanta

By **Elijah R. Freeman**

Despite The Odds

By **Juhnell Morgan**

Good Girl Gone Rogue

By **Manny Black**

Hittaz

Hittaz 2

Hittaz 3

Coldhearted

By **Lou Garden Price, Sr.**

Charge It To The Game

Charge It To The Game 2

A Summer To Remember With My Hitta

Snatched Up By A Hitta

By **Mia Sky**

Thug Me The Right Way
By **DiamondATL & Nai**

BOOKS BY

URBAN AINT DEAD's C.E.O

Elijah R. Freeman

Triggadale

Triggadale 2

Triggadale 3

Tales 4rm Da Dale

The Hottest Summer Ever

Murda Was The Case

Murda Was The Case 2

Murda Was The Case 3

Hittin' Licks For The Holidays: Atlanta

STAY CONNECTED

Follow
Elijah R. Freeman
On Social Media
FB: Elijah R. Freeman
IG: @the_future_of_urban_fiction